Count Flambert's Crime

by G. H. Teed

Illustrated by Val Reading

First published in The Union Jack Library,
Series 2, No. 971, 20 May 1922.

Stillwoods Edition

Stillwoods.Blogspot.Ca

Catalogue Information:
Title: Count Flambert's Crime
Author: G. H. Teed (1881-1938)
Illustrated by: Val Reading
First published anonymously in The Union Jack Library, Series 2, No. 971, 20 May 1922.
This Edition by: Stillwoods, 2021
ISBN Canada: 978-1-989788-81-3
Blog: Stillwoods.Blogspot.Ca
Author Blog: http://ghteed.blogspot.com/
Storefront: http://www.lulu.com/spotlight/lulubook22

https://tinyurl.com/ve25d42s This link should go to a spreadsheet of all known Teed stories. The list is annotated with various information on the stories and my progress with recapturing the work. The library of Teed's stories increases almost weekly. Check at the **Lulu.Com** for the latest arrivals. Search for Teed./drf

Keywords: Sexton Blake, British fictional detective, Tinker, Yvonne Cartier.

Cautionary Note: This series of books by Stillwoods are intended to make the stories of G. H. Teed, born in New Brunswick, Canada, available to collectors and researchers. The editor, or rather digitizer has not altered the original publication.

This story may contain language and racial terms that are not appropriate to today. I apologize for them; I know that the author was using his voice to excite and entertain an adventurous English audience. These works were published from 82 to 110 years ago. Most every work has characters of redeeming ethnicity within.

I hope you enjoy and share these stories; I have.

Doug Frizzle

My thanks to Nico Lorenzutti for his work converting the image pages to text. /drf

A Story of a Double Crime, and one in which the gifted creator of the fascinating Mademoiselle Yvonne excels even his own previous successes. The scene is laid in the mysterious East—in which the writer has travelled widely, and in which he finds a fine field for his special talent. This latest adventure of the famous trio — SEXTON BLAKE, TINKER, and Mlle. YVONNE—will certainly please you. It will grip your interest right from the start.

Huxton Rymer - President
When Greek Meets Greek
At the Turn of the Hour
The Sunken Schooner
The Black Emperor
The Idol's Spell

All available at the lowest price on Lulu.Com. Search for 'Teed'.

ANOTHER COLOURED PICTURE-CARD THIS WEEK! (SEE BELOW.)

THE UNION JACK LIBRARY

2d

EVERY THURSDAY.
No. 971.
May 20th, 1922.

Trooper, Canadian Mounted Police (The "North-West Mounted").

This Splendid Coloured Picture-card, the third in our series depicting **POLICE OF ALL NATIONS** is given **FREE** with this issue.

— :*: —

Are you collecting them? Examine the one enclosed, and then place a standing order for the "U. J."

CONTENTS
of the 8-page
DETECTIVE MAGAZINE
SUPPLEMENT.

— * —

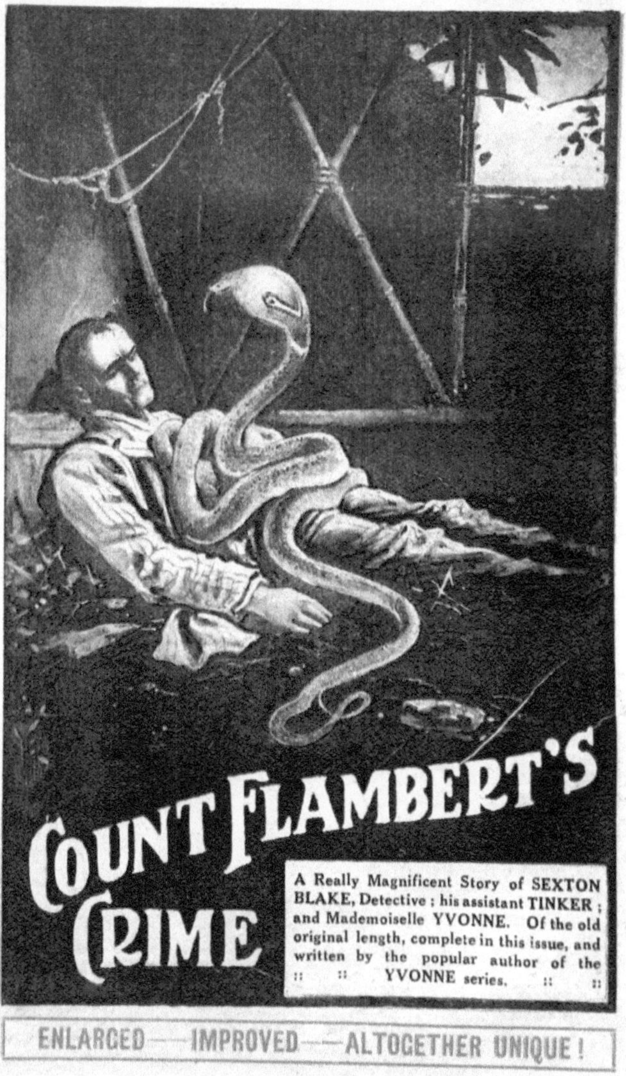

COUNT FLAMBERT'S CRIME

A Really Magnificent Story of SEXTON BLAKE, Detective; his assistant TINKER; and Mademoiselle YVONNE. Of the old original length, complete in this issue, and written by the popular author of the :: :: YVONNE series. :: ::

ENLARGED — IMPROVED — ALTOGETHER UNIQUE!

V

Count Flambert's Crime

A Story of a Double Crime,

and one in which the gifted creator of the fascinating Mademoiselle Yvonne excels even his own previous successes. The scene is laid in the mysterious East—in which the writer has travelled widely, and in which he finds a fine field for his special talent. This latest adventure of the famous trio—SEXTON BLAKE, TINKER, and Mlle. YVONNE—will certainly please you. It will grip your interest right from the start.

U.J.—No. 971.

THE PROLOGUE.

The Paris of the East—The Two Adventurers—When Rogues Fall Out—The House of the Poppy—The Imps of Opium—What the Twisted Eurasian Saw.

CONSIDERING its enormous importance as the gateway to and the seat of government of the great French colonial possessions of Indo-China, it is strange that the wonderful city of Saigon should be so little known to the outside world.

Even in the Far East—in Hong Kong, Shanghai, Bangkok, and Singapore—there are people who have but the vaguest idea of what the busy port is and what it means. And yet among those who know it, it is called the Paris of the East.

Not many years ago Saigon was a dirty, mephitic spot straggling along the banks of the Saigon River, near the mouth. With their marvellous genius for administration, the French have turned it into a beautiful European city, Easternised and planted among the fragrant exotic foliage of the East.

Close to the bank of the river it still displays some remains of the old ugliness, but, once away from the noise and smells of the rice mills and the docks, it opens up into a beautiful arrangement of broad, well-paved boulevards and streets, which are lined with substantially built banks and shops, and attractive-looking houses.

In the very centre of the city, not far from Government House, the French have built a small but very finely proportioned opera house which, like its greater counterpart in Paris, is the centre to which the gayer side of life gravitates.

Facing the square is the pleasant Hotel de l'Europe; and on the other side, shops, astonishingly like those of London or Paris, despite the little Eastern booths of the ubiquitous money changers which are squeezed in between them.

Past that square and on to the main boulevard beyond sweeps all the colour of an Eastern city, and while lacking the deeper intrigue of Canton and the flaming hues of Madras or Mysore, it is, nevertheless, a wonderful pageant of Eastern life.

Beyond the city proper lies a thickly-foliaged suburb, where the French inhabitants have built their villas, and beyond that again, comes the great broad road which links up Saigon with all the rest of Indo-China in the vast sweep of the Mandarin's Road, which is an even finer piece of work than the old Grand Trunk Road of India.

It is just where the villas of the Europeans end, and the native quarter begins, that one begins to feel the deep, pulsating artery of the real East; and, as one gets deeper among the whispering groves of the "quarter," one may lift the curtain and peer upon the secret life which seethes in sinister silence beneath the cloak of outward beauty.

On a hot August night the dining room and the terrace cafe of the Hotel de l'Europe was a blaze of colour and movement. Every table was occupied, and above the clatter of dishes and the clink of glasses rose the ceaseless murmur of a dozen different languages.

Saigon itself was there, young men and old men, and family parties seeking relief from the heat beneath the wide electric fans which whirred overhead. There had been, too, an influx of passengers from the great French mail-steamer, Amiral Lebon, which had just arrived, bringing a full quota of passengers from Haiphong, Hanoi, and Hue, officers in brilliant uniforms, police officials from the Hanoi department in Annam, planters, business men, wives and daughters, and a small sprinkling of the type of adventurer one meets in every port of the East.

The square was brightly lighted, and along the boulevard in front of the hotel passed a steady stream of motor-cars, ancient looking carriages, and those Saigonese who might not seek amusement in the somewhat exclusive precincts of the hotel.

At one end of the terrace, at a small marble-topped table, a little removed from the others, sat two men.

They had arrived an hour before by the mail steamer from Haiphong, but, unlike the majority of the passengers, they were not continuing on to Marseilles on furlough. They were to remain in Saigon for the present, and their reason was a very simple one—insufficient funds to carry them any great distance beyond.

They were both French, and, although they did not know it, their departure from Haiphong had been a move of safety. One was tall and somewhat spare, with close-shaven, hard features—a man one would say in the early thirties.

His companion was small and weedy-looking, with sallow, unhealthy skin, dark, shifty eyes, and a loose mouth which revealed both weakness and criminal instinct. The events which led up to their departure from Haiphong for Saigon was but a story which could be oft-told on the China coast.

They were adventurers who had "worked" the coast from Singapore to Shanghai in an attempt to secure the big prize which the type is always seeking.

A little card-sharping in Singapore, gambling in the Chinese joints of Bangkok, a month at the tables at the Monte Carlo of the East in the Portuguese possession of Macao at the mouth of the Canton River, where they had a run of luck; then the lure which has at one time or another attracted every crook in the East—the lure of the fabulous golden treasure of the ancient Annamese kings which rests in the palace fortress at Hue.

From Haiphong the pair had worked along to Hanoi, and so on to Hue. They had made a survey of the position there, and in the deeps of the native town opposite the palace they had planned their attempt.

But they had not counted on the far-reaching power and subtlety of M. Dubois, the French Commissaire of Police at Hanoi. From the very moment of their departure they had been trailed, and on the night when, with a big dance at the Residency, they had considered the time opportune, they had made their attempt to enter the sacred palace of the ancient Annamese, they had been very quietly "gathered in."

M. Dubois was apologetic and sympathetic, but behind his suave protests both Lacroix and Journet knew a will of iron lay concealed.

So back to Hanoi they had made their way, poorer and considerably wiser. Annam was closed to them. Hong Kong had been worked out. Manila was not auspicious at the time. Shanghai would give them the same sort of reception. Where should they go?

A stocktaking of finances decided them on Saigon as a start. And so this pair of rogues ambled forth, and by the mail steamer came into Saigon to see how little they might sow, and how much they might reap.

But that all was not quite right between them would have been discovered that night at the Hotel de l'Europe, in Saigon, if one could have overheard their conversation as they sat at the table on the veranda terrace.

Lacroix, the taller, more sinister of the two, was speaking in a low tone, with scarcely any movement of the lips. His voice carried to the ears of his companion only.

"You may say what you will, my friend." he was saying, "but I tell you that I know you got the sapphire in Hue. You have been cunning, and have concealed it well; but I know, I tell you, is that the act of a friend of a comrade?"

The shifty eyes of the other fell before the direct glare of Lacroix.

"I have told you before, mon brave, that you are mistaken. I got no sapphire in Hue, or any place else."

"You lie!" remarked Lacroix. And although the words were spoken in the same low tone they cut on Journet's hearing with a threat that made him move uneasily in his seat. "You have a poor memory, my friend. Kulai-Tui, the little Annamese girl at the hotel in Hanoi, whom you have perhaps forgotten, told me that she had seen you fondling and admiring a stone of sapphire blue. Can you deny it?"

"No, I have not forgotten. If Kulai-Tui said that, she lied! I had no stone; I have no stone."

Lacroix shrugged.

"Our agreement was a partnership agreement," he remarked. "By keeping that stone to yourself you have broken the bond which bound us. Convince me that you have never possessed it—that you do not possess now. That is all I ask."

"You speak of a partnership agreement!" snarled the small man. "What about your winnings in Macao? Did you share those with me?"

"No, because you were making a fool of yourself. It was because I kept a strong rein on you that you finally won there. But that aside, your very protest proves that you have lied to me about the sapphire. Very well, my friend, we will say no more about it. I need you, and you need me, at present. As soon as we have brought something to a head here we shall dissolve partnership. Are you agreed?"

"As you will!" muttered Journet.

"Let us not quarrel," went on Lacroix. "Myself, I feel like the pipe. Are you agreeable?"

The eyes of the other lit up.

"Yes," he said eagerly. "Let us get out of this place."

Lacroix nodded, and summoned the waiter. He paid the score, and the pair rose.

Passing between the tables on the terrace, they emerged upon the street, where Lacroix hailed one of the ancient fiacres which stood in the shadow of the opera house.

As Journet stepped in, Lacroix gave the address which the shabby driver seemed to understand well enough. The carriage rattled away from the square, and, turning to the left, took its way along a street running parallel to the rear of the hotel.

From there its course went by turning after turning, until it reached the chief suburb, where the night air was heavy with the scent of foliage and flowers. Gradually the occasional street lamp became a rarity, and then, as they came to a thick grove of areca palms, the way was lit only by the myriad stars overhead.

The grove of arecas proved to be a plantation rather than a haphazard collection of trees, and in reality it was the boundary point which marked the end of the European quarter, and the beginning of the whispering groves of the native district. After passing the arecas, the fiacre turned to the right.

The two passengers felt a sudden jolting which told them the well-made road had been left, and, indeed, they soon turned into a lane so narrow that the palms appeared to meet overhead. Through the foliage on each side they caught the occasional gleam of a light—a fugitive spark that shone for a moment, then disappeared.

The very air seemed pregnant with mystery and intrigue, with the scented night breeze which droned with the rustling of the palm fronds overhead the secrets which were whispered by a thousand pairs of lips.

They were still in the deep shadow of the overhanging trees when the carriage came to a stop.

On the right the shrubbery was so thick that nothing could be seen. On the left a high bamboo gate could be dimly discerned, set in a dense hedge. But no light came from beyond.

Lacroix and Journet descended. Lacroix paid the "cocher," who drove off at once. In a few moments the night and the soft earth had taken him beyond sight and sound.

Lacroix led the way towards the bamboo gate. As they reached it he gave a low whistle.

With startling suddenness the gate opened inwards a little, and the sinister features a low-caste Tongkinese appeared. Lacroix spoke a few words to him, and after further scrutiny of the visitors, the Asiatic opened the gate wider.

The two Frenchmen entered, and the gate closed silently after them. The Celestial sank to the ground, blending with the shadows. Lacroix and Journet went cautiously up a path which was heavy with the scent of the hibiscus flower.

5

At first it seemed that they might have been in some lost path in the heart of the jungle—a path that began nowhere and ended nowhere. Now and then mysterious scufflings sounded on either side, and Journet peered nervously about him.

Once he shivered, and almost hesitated as though filled with a sudden premonition of danger. But Lacroix kept on, and Journet stumbled after him.

Then, just ahead, the dark bulk of a bungalow villa loomed up. It gave no sign of light, but Lacroix, who moved with a certainty that told of a previous acquaintance with the place, felt for and found the three shallow steps that led to the veranda.

Mounting them, he crossed the veranda, and fumbled about until he found a heavy rattan curtain which was hung over the door. Thrusting his hand beneath, he rapped sharply, and waited.

Nothing happened for a full minute, and then a light fell upon them with such disconcerting abruptness that Journet jumped. It seemed to come from a spot farther down the veranda, and played deliberately over their features.

Lacroix faced it unblinkingly, while the other shifted uneasily. The light went out as suddenly as it had come, and the next moment the door behind the rattan curtain was opened. Lacroix passed behind the curtain, and entered the room, followed by Journet.

The apartment into which they stepped was a most unprepossessing one. It was small, and furnished in a ludicrous travesty of a middle-class French villa in the suburbs of Marseilles or Paris. In the centre of the room was a square table covered with a red-plush cloth. The chairs had obviously been brought from France, and the pictures on the walls were coloured lithographs of French patriotic subjects.

Dirty bits of cheap lace seemed to be hung in almost every available place, and even draped the backs of the chairs. Were it not for the few pieces of bamboo furniture scattered about, and a lacquered cabinet in one corner, the room would have given no suggestion of the East, and certainly one would be little inclined to associate mystery or intrigue with that tawdry and vulgarly furnished room.

But not so with he who had opened the door, for a more villainous countenance it would have been difficult to find.

Even the loose, criminal features of Journet appeared to possess a certain refinement and breeding in comparison. The man was short and held himself in a bent, twisted way that told of spinal curvature. His body was small and grotesque-looking; his arms extraordinarily long, while his head appeared to be enormous in contrast. The features were those of a half-caste—the eyes oblique and truly Oriental, while the nose and chin were distinctly European.

But what gave the creature the most sinister touch of all was the bald scalp. Not a single vestige of hair could be seen, the whole pate being as smooth and naked as the proverbial billiard ball.

He said no word as he closed the door after his visitors; but when he had secured the latch he motioned them to seats. Lacroix made a gesture for Journet to be seated, and himself took a chair near the table. Their host, in the meantime, had crossed to the lacquered cabinet.

He opened what had appeared to be part of the solid side of the article, but was reality a secret panel. From the compartment which was revealed he took a bottle and two glasses. He placed them on the table, and Journet leant forward as he saw that the bottle contained absinthe.

The Eurasian crossed to the cabinet once more, and this time he brought a carafe of water, some lumps of sugar, and a perforate spoon. Lacroix took up the glasses, and resting the spoon across the edges of one on the glasses, laid a lump of sugar in the bowl. He poured a generous quantity the absinthe into the glass; then, taking up the carafe, allowed the water to trickle slowly upon the lump of sugar, after which it dripped through the holes in the bowl of the spoon into the absinthe beneath.

It took several minutes before he was satisfied with the amount that had gone into the mixture, but when it was finished to his liking he handed the glass to Journet, and proceeded to mix the second one for himself. This done they drank, and then only did the Eurasian speak. He made use of the harsh patois of his kind.

"It is a long time since you have been here, monsieur," he said, addressing Lacroix.

"It is many months," replied the Frenchman. "I have been in the north in Hanoi."

"Yes, I have heard. I have heard, too, that monsieur and his friend failed to secure the treasure of the Annamese kings."

It did not seem to strike that the half-caste should have known so soon of their attempt and failure on the palace treasure at Hue. He knew the East too well to wonder at the rapidity with which bazaar whisperings travel. He just nodded.

"Yes. There have been too many attempts lately. It is too well guarded."

"And M. le Commissaire at Hanoi is too careful," supplemented the Eurasian. "But why have monsieur and his friend come here to-night?"

"We want to smoke," responded Lacroix curtly.

"And monsieur's friend?"

"Yes. He is all right. I will vouch for him."

The Eurasian nodded, and, crossing the room, pressed a part of the wall, immediately revealing another secret panel. He slid this to one side, and beckoned to the two Frenchmen. Lacroix led the way, and Journet followed.

They passed through the opening into a room which was in startling contrast to the one they had just left. It was long and narrow, and apparently formed the "ell" of the villa. The walls were hung with Annamese and Tongkinese mats on which were weird representations of birds and animals. The floor was covered with the same sort of mats.

The only lighting was from a heavy filigree brass lamp that hung from the ceiling. It had about a score of narrow grooves round the edge of the bowl, from each of which dangled a wick, the other end of which rested in coconut oil.

Along each side of the room were ranged, alternately, first a low rattan couch, then a small tabourette, then a couch accompanied by another table. There were six couches on each side, and, at the moment, four of these were occupied.

On the small tabourette which had been set between each couch were all the implements needed for opium-smoking—the pipe, with its thick stem, and tiny hole at the mouth end, and the flat top of the bowl, over the centre hole of which the "pill" would be rolled and heated; the little spirit-lamp for heating the tip of the needle, and a small tin of prepared opium of the consistency of soft putty and the colour of dark resin.

Lacroix gazed with interest at the four figures lying on the couches.

Near at hand he saw a man who looked incongruous in those surroundings. He was lying on the first couch on the left, and had, apparently, already reached the stage of deep sleep and drugged dreams, for he was tossing restlessly and muttering from time to time. He appeared to be about forty years of age, well clad in a fine silk suit, although his linen and tie had become disarranged during his debauch. His head was finely proportioned, and his black beard and moustache were neatly trimmed.

Lacroix smiled a little as he saw him, for he recognised the prostrate one as a prominent planter, and one highly respected in the colony. He made no remark, however, but allowed his gaze to travel over the others.

One man, whom he recognised as a well-known waster who was maintained in Saigon by a disgusted family in Paris, was at the moment rolling and heating the pill with a shaky hand. It was obvious that he was on the verge of collapse. Another was a stout Tongkinese whom Lacroix had never seen before, but who was taking his pipe coolly and deliberately. The fourth was a shabbily-dressed man who looked British, and, as a matter of fact, he was. Like the men on the first couch, he was in a deep sleep.

All four were lying on the left side of the room, but Lacroix and Journet chose the two first couches on the right. As Lacroix lay down on the first, and Journet followed suit, the Eurasian brought two tins of opium and opened them. Then he lit the spirit-lamps, and, without a word, went back to the front room, closing the panel after him.

Lacroix and Journet were both confirmed "smokers," and neither of them showed the touch of the amateur as he took out a little of the sticky drug from the tin, and, twirling it slowly above the flame, moulded it and rounded it to his satisfaction. Perhaps six or seven minutes were consumed before each was satisfied with his pill, then, as the drug smouldered, they held it over the small hole at the top of the flat bowl, and, placing the mouthpiece between the lips, inhaled deeply.

Only a few inhalations did they gain from each "pill," but it seemed to awaken a desire for more; and neither man seemed impatient at the time it took to prepare for those brief seconds of enjoyment. On the contrary, the process seemed to give them a lazy enjoyment of anticipation.

Thus it went until each had smoked his seventh pipe. Neither had spoken a word during that time, nor had they even glanced in the direction of the other opium-takers.

By this time the young French waster had collapsed, but the fat Tongkinese was as collected as ever. It was when Lacroix and Journet were beginning to prepare their eighth pipe that the Tongkinese laid down his pipe and got heavily to his feet. He lumbered along towards the panel by which they had entered. It opened as he approached, as though the Eurasian keeper of the "joint" had instinctively guessed his coming. Neither Lacroix nor Journet knew that the occupants of the smoking-room were under the constant surveillance of the Eurasian through a secret peephole near the panel.

The panel slid to after the Tongkinese, and silence reigned once more in that place of drug debauchery.

Lacroix and Journet were now the only two who were awake, although Journet was beginning to show signs of drowsiness.

The effect on Lacroix had been different. Instead of being overcome by sleep, his eyes glittered with unnatural vigour. His skin seemed to have become more tightly drawn across his cheek-bones, while his mouth was harder and straighter than ever. He looked evil and dangerous. And if Journet could only have guessed the drug-painted thoughts that were surging in the mind of his companion, he would have used his few remaining wits to get out of the place.

There were a few persons who knew just how dangerous Lacroix could be, and while the Eurasian was one of those, Journet was not. In their argument that night at the Hotel de l'Europe, what Lacroix had accused his partner of had not been without foundation.

By simple sneak-thievery, Journet had gained possession of a sapphire in Hanoi, and the information had been communicated to Lacroix by an Annamese girl in the hotel there. Journet had lied in denying the possession of the stone, and had given himself away badly under Lacroix's cross-examination. But while Lacroix had apparently dismissed the matter from his mind, he had by no means done so.

He was determined that before the night went by the sapphire should pass into his keeping.

Under the urge of the insidious drug, this determination had slowly changed to a venomous hatred of Journet, and as the distorted mind-pictures assailed him his eyes shone with a hard glitter that revealed the dangerous fire which was burning within. But with it, too, was the cunning which the drug also gives to its devotees, and not for a single moment did the befuddled Journet suspect that his companion was mentally plotting against him.

On the ninth pipe Journet fell back with a sigh, babbling foolishly as the kaleidoscopic imagery of the drug passed before his inflamed senses in a whirling sunset of unbelievable colour and movement, while on his own couch Lacroix was rolling his tenth pill with a steady hand.

But his mind was filled with a mad riot of dancing figures which advanced and retreated, which scowled upon him and mocked him, which jeered at him and nagged him with a persistency that drove him frantic.

Ceaselessly the demon within intoned its insults:

"You are a fool! Journet has defrauded you. Journet has betrayed you. Journet has kept the sapphire for his own purposes. He will sell it, and reap all the benefit. The sapphire may not be the only thing he has!"

Then the swaying, dancing figures of the mocking imps would swing about in a mad whirl of fiendish glee, while the tortured brain reeled beneath the impact of the opium's phantom pageant.

One persistent demon leered at Lacroix from behind a great tree. His talon-like fingers pointed and twisted in derision. His scalp moved backwards and forwards like that of an ape. Then he broke into a shrill cackle of running insult—or so the distorted fancy of Lacroix believed:

"Journet may have many stones on him. If he got one sapphire in Hanoi, he may have got more. Who knows? He was away alone many times. He has kept with you just until he lulls your suspicions and manages to get away. Take him now—take him now! You have him in your power. Throttle the truth from him! He is at your mercy! Tear from him the stones, the wealth of which he has stolen from you! Look at him now—he is in the heights of the gods. He is laughing at you for a fool! Take him now—take him n-o-w, NOW!"

Outwardly, Lacroix was steady enough, but by the time he had finished his twelfth pipe the pupils of his eyes had widened until they looked like two glittering pieces of rubbed coal. His skin had turned to a greyish yellow, and he was panting in a short, sharp, whistling manner as though he had run a great distance. And all the time the imps and gargoyles jeered at him and drove him on.

At last he turned and bent his glittering gaze on Journet.

The other lay back, his loose mouth wide open, babbling happily. He appeared to Lacroix to be laughing in evil triumph. It was the one thing needed to snap the last thread of control which bound his tortured brain to sanity. As silently as a snake he twisted his body and slithered off the couch.

One stealthy step brought him beside Journet.

His hands were perfectly steady as he slipped them beneath his companion's coat and began to feel cautiously for the hidden sapphires—for it was of many sapphires he now thought.

He did not know that each movement was watched by a pair of sloe-black eyes which gazed impassively through the peephole near the panel. Nor, knowing, would he have cared now.

Suddenly, beneath Journet's collar, he felt something hard. It was the sapphire which Journet had hung in a little bag about his neck. With infinite caution he unbuttoned the other's shirt and tried to get hold of the cord which held the tiny sack.

But those same imps of madness must have turned their attention to Journet now, for even as Lacroix's fingers sought and found the cord, Journet gave a cry, and began to struggle, his eyes opening in a wild stare as he saw that the shadowy menace of Lacroix which he had seen in his dreams was stark reality.

As he screamed out Lacroix drove him back with a crashing fist, then his hand went to his hip-pocket, and he drew out a small, vicious-looking automatic. Raising it, he aimed; then the silence of the smoking-room was shattered by two crashes as Lacroix pulled the trigger.

Journet's eyes widened in helpless terror for the barest fraction of an instant, then he dropped back with two bullets in his heart.

Lacroix straightened up, and looked behind him. None of the three other inmates had been aroused by the two shots. Each was sleeping just as before, although the man near the door was now moving restlessly. It was on him that Lacroix's gaze rested longest.

The hard glitter of his eyes changed to a deep cunning as he looked and, with an almost childish smile of glee, he moved across the room until he stood over the prostrate man. Bending down gently, he insinuated the automatic beneath the hand of the other closing the fingers over the butt.

Then he backed away until he had reached Journet's couch again. He had no difficulty now in securing the little sack containing the sapphire. He slipped it in his pocket and stood up. Although his skin was still drawn tight, and his eyes were still wide with the drug. Lacroix was perfectly clear in his mind.

He knew that he must get away.

His thoughts went to the mail steamer which lay in port. If he could reach that, and continue on to Singapore, he would be all right. He turned, and then, as he started towards the panel, he raised his eyes to see, standing just inside the opening, the twisted figure of the Eurasian.

END OF PROLOGUE.

As Journet screamed out, Lacroix drove him back on the opium-den mattress with a crashing fist. Then his hand went to his hip-pocket, and he drew out a vicious looking automatic. (*Prologue.*)

In the Manilla Hotel Blake on Holiday—An Introduction And An Interloper.

IT was a very merry, congenial party that was gathered at a large tea-table at one end of the veranda lounge of the Manila Hotel. Those at other tables sent more than one glance of interest in its direction, for although some of the party had landed in Manila only that morning, their names were already on the lips of the other guests of the hotel. The rumour that they had come from the beautiful white steam yacht, that could be seen lying at anchor on the deep blue waters of the bay, had been sufficient to create deep interest; and when the names of the tall, rather spare, distinguished-looking man and the slim, beautiful girl, who were in the party, had leaked out, this interest was increased tremendously.

And then, when Stephen Barclay, the American mining and oil millionaire, had greeted the new arrivals warmly, and had joined the party, all sorts of rumours began to be whispered.

It was perhaps natural that what was apparently a long and earnest conversation between Stephen Barclay and the famous criminologist, Sexton Blake, should give rise to such rumours. But those who passed them on, with additions and trimmings of their own, would have been somewhat abashed if they had known that the topic under such serious discussion between the two men was not the intriguing subject of crime, but the merits and demerits of different makes of golf-balls in the tropics.

But while the interest of the men was centred on Blake and the millionaire, that of the feminine element was concentrated on the beautiful Mademoiselle Cartier. Her frock was a wonderful, filmy creation that they knew in some mysterious way that can never be understood by mere man—was the last word of the Parisian dressmakers. She was chatting gaily with Betty Barclay, the millionaire's only child, and the apple of his eye. She was a delightfully attractive specimen of young girlhood, and at least one of the party appeared to have accepted this fact without the slightest reservation.

That one was a sturdy, well-set-up, sunburned young man, who seemed to be having considerable success in his efforts to entertain Mademoiselle Yvonne and the girl; though it must be confessed that

Tinker, for it was he, had evolved a most weird and wonderful detective tale for the edification of Miss Barclay when she had insisted that he tell her some of his experiences.

The party was completed by an elderly gentleman, whose well-trimmed, pointed white beard and genial, easy manner marked him as a man of the world in the real sense. The casual observer would have put him down as simply a gentleman of leisure, travelling for amusement, or perhaps a retired official of the Diplomatic Service. The individual in question would have drawled out, if asked, that he found it quite strenuous enough being uncle to Mademoiselle Yvonne, and it must be confessed that at times Yvonne led Graves an anxious time.

From the cool, wide, shady veranda of the hotel there was a clear view across the open green, which stretched to the docks, and then beyond the great blue bay which undulated lazily beneath the afternoon sun. Immediately across from them was the fine building of the American Army and Navy Club, and, beyond, a stretch of palms which hid the modern town from view. To the right, and lying between the hotel and the piers was the golf-links; while beyond that again was the old Spanish town, whose ancient walls and fort still exist, and where the Spanish soldiers stood watching on that fatal day when the American fleet, under Dewey, annihilated the Spanish squadron.

Away to the south-west, with their graceful lines standing out in sharp silhouette against the deep blue of the sky, were the twin wireless towers, with a definite sending radius of seven thousand miles, and receiving power of even greater distance. They can pick up Sydney, or the Eiffel Tower, or the west coast of America with equal facility, and, on occasion, have been known to pick up Washington clearly.

Away to the east, beyond the new town, rose the hills—bank upon bank of bluey-green lush jungle, away on the crest of which lay Bagnio, the hill station. It was this place, in fact, which formed the subject of discussion between Sexton Blake and Stephen Barclay, for at Bagnio are the finest golf links in the Philippines, and both Blake and the millionaire were considering a brief visit there.

Blake and Tinker were Yvonne's guests on the Fleur-de-Lys.

The yacht had been in dry dock since Yvonne's previous cruise in the Far East the year before, but as soon as it had been relaunched, she had planned another cruise, and would take "no" from neither Blake nor the lad.

The result was that Blake had wound up his most pressing affairs in London, and had turned over the rest to Gordon Lindsay, his Montreal correspondent, who had come across to England to carry on at Baker Street during Blake's absence.

Both Blake and Tinker needed a long holiday, for they had had a very strenuous time of it during the previous few months, with scarcely any change from the gruelling routine of work. And it was with the fixed determination that nothing smacking in the least of business should be allowed to break in upon their holiday, that they had joined the Fleur-de-Lys at Plymouth.

Blake had even gone to the extent of instructing Lindsay that no letters were to be forwarded; and up to the time they reached Manila this programme had been carried out, and they had made a very lazy and enjoyable voyage of it. After leaving England they had stopped for a day at Gibraltar, and, following that, a day at Malta. From Malta they had made the direct run to Port Said, where Blake took the opportunity of running up to Cairo to see an old friend, although the others remained on the yacht. From Port Said they had passed through the Canal, had remained only four hours at Suez; then, with all fans going, had slipped through the Red Sea as quickly as possible.

They had not put into Colombo on the outward voyage, intending to stop there on the way back. But they had spent a couple of days at Singapore, after which they had run across to Batavia and Surabaja.

Followed a lazy cruise through the Sulu Sea, past the Moluccas, and then along the fringe of Cebu and into Manila Bay. They intended remaining at least four days in Manila, and possibly longer. After that the yacht would make for Hong Kong, from which place Blake wanted to revisit Canton and Macao.

If no urgent cables were waiting in Hong Kong, it had been half decided to go across to Haiphong and Saigon in French IndoChina, and then homeward.

Blake, Yvonne, Graves, and Tinker had all come ashore that morning, leaving Captain Vaughan the whole day in which to spruce up the yacht and to take in oil for the engines—for Yvonne had had the Fleur-de-Lys converted into an oil burner.

They had "done" the old town, the fort, the cathedral, the old chambers of the Inquisition, and then had motored along the Escolta and through the new town. They had lunched at the Manila Hotel, and it was there Blake had run into Stephen Barclay.

As it was too hot to play golf before tea, they had sat beneath the electric fans on the wide veranda, chatting, until tea-time, after which Blake and the millionaire proposed making a round of the pretty, but not very difficult, links adjoining the hotel.

Tinker, Yvonne, and Betty Barclay were going with a couple of young American naval officers to a dance at the club, and Graves had elected to remain where he was, sipping cool drinks and watching the life about him.

Blake and Barclay had just risen to pick up their clubs and stroll across to the first tee, when suddenly Barclay drew up with a sharp exclamation.

"Excuse me a moment, Blake, please," he said. "There is an old friend of mine who has just come up the steps. He must have arrived by the Pacific mail steamer that has just docked."

Blake nodded, and glanced in the direction towards which the millionaire was hastening. He saw a middle-aged gentleman, of distinctly French appearance, coming up the steps of the veranda, and beside him was a dark-haired, pretty girl of seventeen or eighteen. Blake lighted a cigarette and strolled back to the table, where Tinker was still carrying on a bantering conversation with Betty Barclay.

"You take my advice, Miss Barclay," he said with a smile, "and use a little salt with what you are hearing from this young man. I know that look in his eye of old."

The girl turned a pair of wide eyes on Blake.

"Oh, but, Mr. Blake!" she responded. "I think it is just too wonderful for anything the way he tracks people down. He has just been telling me about the most thrilling struggle in which he had to hold a man with one hand, shoot at another man with the other, and strike another with the other, and—"

Tinker grinned sheepishly under Blake's look.

"Excuse me a moment, Miss Barclay," said Blake, "but all the others' and anothers' are rather confusing. How many hands was he using?"

"He had to hold a man with one hand, shoot at another man with the other, and strike another with the other." parroted the girl, her eyes widely innocent.

Blake glanced at her quizzically, then smiled and turned away.

"I am afraid that is too much for me," he said. But as he got out of earshot he murmured: "I'm blest, but I do believe the girl is spoofing Tinker, and he thinks he is spoofing her."

Just then he saw Stephen Barclay coming towards him, accompanied by the tall, thin, bearded Frenchman and the young girl, whom Blake fancied must be his daughter. This was confirmed a few seconds later when Barclay introduced them as Count Rene Flambert and Mademoiselle Flambert.

Blake bowed, and made some conventional expression of pleasure, then took them across to the table where the others sat. He introduced them all round, and Yvonne made a place for the girl beside her, while Graves turned his attention to the count. Leaving them all thus engaged, Blake and Barclay finally got away. As they strolled through the gardens in front of the hotel, Blake asked for information about the new arrival.

"I can't tell you a great deal about him," responded the American, "although I have known him slightly for a good many years. You remember, Blake, I used to be director on the China Coast for the National Oil Co. of New York. It was in those days that I first met him.

"I always liked him, although, when he was much younger, there was a wild streak in him that used to break out on occasion. We had oil installations along the coast all the way down from Shanghai to Bangkok, and, together with Hong Kong and Manila, that made up my district. The Indian section controlled things east as far as Singapore.

"I was out on inspection a great deal, and used to get to Saigon quite often. That was where I met Flambert. He had a big plantation there, and appeared to be very well off. I was out at his place once, I fancy his wife must have died several years ago, for I never saw her, and he never spoke of her. He did speak freely, though, of his daughter, whom you saw to-day, but who was then at school in France. It seems that I heard, either in Hong Kong or Canton, that he had left Saigon, but no one seemed to know where he had gone. I took it for granted that, on the daughter's account, he had probably returned to France—until I saw him to-day. I don't know what they can be doing in Manila, unless they are just 'doing' the East, as we are. What did you think of him?"

"I didn't have much time to judge but what I did see of him I liked. At the same time, he struck me as a man who is in a distinctly nervous condition. I should not think this sort of a holiday would be the right thing for that."

"You have sharp eyes. Now that you mention it, I noticed, too, that he had a worried air. Perhaps he was hit financially during the war. Well, here we are at the first tee. Shall we toss, or will you take the honour?"

"Your honour," rejoined Blake, as he surveyed the dirty array of young Filipinos who had bobbed up from apparently nowhere. They selected two of the dirtiest as caddies and shooed the others away. Then, in the seriousness of the game, everything else was forgotten.

It has already been stated that the golf links lay between the hotel and the shore. The first nine holes carried them across the road which led from the harbour to the new town, almost to the American Club; then they came back on the other side of the hotel, and finished off in the direction of the old walled town.

It was a glorious day for playing. Although there was not a cloud in the sky, and the sun blazed down warmly, the evening breeze had begun.

Out in the wide, beautiful bay the lazy blue had been flecked to strips of white. Underfoot the turf was soft and springy. To the distance the mountains loomed in deepening purple, with faint wisps of white trailing down the valleys, where the night mist was gathering. Close at hand stood the two great buildings—the hotel and the club—that marked the efficient present, and, in grim contrast, was the cold, moss-grown grey of the old walls which had known so much of the bigoted past.

Both Blake and the millionaire were in good form, and, as they reached the ninth tee, which would carry them across the road past the hotel, they were exactly even, Barclay having managed to halve the eighth with a long putt.

Blake drove first, making a good start straight along the fairway, over the road, and just clearing the turf bunker to the right of the hotel. Barclay sliced a little and got a bad lie in the rough. He laughed good-naturedly, and they had just started to walk along when they saw a group coming across the grass towards them.

"Hallo!" exclaimed Blake. "They are just going to the club now to dance."

They waited until the party had reached them, then, telling their scores, they started on. It was then that Count Flambert detached himself and joined the golfers.

"I hope you don't mind," he said, "but I am afraid I am too old for dancing. I will finish the course with you if I may."

"By all means," chorused Blake and Barclay,

And so it was that the count began to walk round with them.

They had played to the thirteenth green, and Barclay was trying a particularly difficult putt. Blake was standing well at one side, talking in a low tone to the count, when he paused in the midst of what he was saying and gazed curiously at the Frenchman.

It had suddenly dawned on Blake that the latter had not been listening to a single word he had been saying, and, not only that but he was gazing over Blake's shoulder with a fixed stare, that, under any other conditions, Blake would have described with just one word—fear.

But what could there be to hold the count rigid with such an emotion there on the links that sunny afternoon? Blake turned slowly and looked in the direction where the other's attention had been fixed. As he did so, he saw a man swinging leisurely across the grass towards them, and, on his drawing nearer, Blake recognised him as a man he had seen about the hotel that day.

Another Introduction—An Unpleasant Surprise for Lacroix—What Captain Vaughan had to Say.

THE newcomer was tall and spare in figure, with dark hair, and prominent features. But for his eyes, the face would have been strong, for the nose had character enough, and the mouth was firm, though cruel. The eyes, however, were hard, blue, and glittering.

Blake knew only too well what that meant, and, even at first sight of the man earlier in the day, he had stamped him as a coast adventurer of the type that would dare a good deal, and who could be a dangerous customer.

Blake turned back to find that the count had apparently recovered his self-possession. Barclay, having missed his putt, had strolled across to wait until Blake had made his play. He arrived just about the same time that the stranger reached them. The latter held out his hand to the count with a smile.

"My dear count," he said, in tones a little too hearty and a little too loud! "What a delightful surprise! I had no idea you were in Manila. I only got in this morning myself. You are looking fit. And how is Mademoiselle Flambert?"

The count shook hands briefly and replied that he was well. But he made no reference to the state of his daughter's health. Then he turned and presented the newcomer to Blake and the millionaire.

"Mr. Barclay—Mr. Blake, let me introduce Monsieur Lacroix."

"Delighted, Mr. Barclay—Mr. Blake!" murmured Lacroix easily. "I have had the pleasure of seeing you before, Mr. Barclay, but have never had the honour of meeting you."

"And wouldn't have had it now if the count could have got out of it," thought Blake, as he gave a stiff bow and turned to address his ball.

The millionaire, who had seen nothing of the effect Lacroix's arrival had had on the count, saw no reason for being frigid with the former. Like Blake, he was a student of men, and, in the one before him, he recognised what he had not seen for some years—the coast adventurer of the polished type—a type for which Barclay had a good-natured tolerance when he was in the East, but which he considered anathema back in New York.

Blake holed out, and, when Barclay had followed suit, they picked up their balls and walked across to the next tee. The count and Lacroix kept beside them until they drove off; then, as Blake bent to choose an iron from his bag, he caught a few words of a remark which Lacroix was making to the count.

Those words were— "I prefer now, but to-night will do—"

There was a curt, peremptory note in Lacroix's voice which puzzled Blake a little. It was in such distinct variance to the hearty words he had uttered before that Blake felt the contrast most unpleasantly. Moreover, it was not the usual tone a younger man would ordinarily use towards a man of the count's years, nor of his rank.

Blake realised that it was, in a way, none of his business; but, nevertheless, he did not propose for a single moment that their game should be upset by this stranger. He straightened up with an iron in his hand, and gazed towards where Lacroix stood. The latter caught the expression in Blake's eyes, and flushed.

"You will pardon me. Monsieur Lacroix," said Blake quietly, "but I must ask you to be good enough not to talk during a stroke unless you are out of hearing."

"A thousand apologies, Mr. Blake!" exclaimed Lacroix, "I have been rude and thoughtless. It was only my delight at seeing my old friend again."

"Liar!" muttered Blake, as he turned away.

As he played the iron shot Blake did not notice the slowly gathering look of concentration in Lacroix's eyes. Nor did he hear his words as he turned to Count Flambert and said quickly:

"Blake—Blake! What Blake is he? His face seems familiar in a way to me, but I can't place him."

The count had started across to join Barclay.

"Did you ever hear of Sexton Blake?" he asked.

"Sexton—" Lacroix's expression suddenly changed.

"Well, that is he," rejoined the count dryly.

Lacroix gave a low whistle, and screwed up his eyes. He regarded first the now distant Blake, then he fixed his eyes on the back of the count.

"Sexton Blake!" he muttered. "Now what the deuce does that mean? Flambert seems friendly enough with him. I wonder if he will be fool enough to tell him anything? Or perhaps he has done so already. Blake didn't seem over keen to talk to me. But Flambert wouldn't dare! He knows what would happen to him if he did. And even for his daughter's sake he would keep his mouth shut.

"At the same time, I don't like this man Blake getting friendly with him. I shall have to see to it that they are kept apart. And I must find out, too, just when Blake arrived here, and how long he is going to stay. I have tapped this tree too long now to have things go wrong. I must bring Flambert to time without further delay. Once I clinch him tonight, I can snap my fingers at Sexton Blake or any other interfering busybody. But I don't like him hanging about, and that's a fact."

For the rest of the game Lacroix devoted himself to watching the millionaire's play, while Count Flambert stayed close by Blake. They finished with Blake two up, and then started across towards the hotel for the inevitable cooling drink at the "nineteenth hole."

They had just finished, when, on coming out from the bar, Blake saw the stocky, white-clad figure of Captain Vaughan coming along the veranda, looking inquiringly from side to side. Blake hailed the commander of the yacht, and they seated themselves at a table while the thirsty mariner quaffed a huge mug of cool ale.

"I came ashore to find out what the plans were for to-night, Mr. Blake," he said, putting down the mug with a sigh.

"We have decided to remain ashore." answered Blake. "I think Mademoiselle Yvonne has a letter ready for her maid about the things she wants. Tinker and I packed a couple of bags before we came ashore, in case this should be decided on, so they can be thrown into the launch. There is a dance on at the roof-garden here to-night, and from what I can gather Tinker and Mademoiselle Yvonne have made up a party with some young folks they have met here."

"All right, Mr. Blake. I'll see that everything is sent across in the launch. I had better wait here and take the note to the maid. Is my owner in the hotel?"

"No, captain, she is over at the club. Some of the naval officers are giving an afternoon dance there; but I expect they will be back at any moment now. I—"

Blake broke off in the middle of a remark for the second time that day, and for the same reason the expression on his listener's face. But on the features of Captain Vaughan there was no look of fear; instead, he was frowning in a puzzled way.

"I beg your pardon, Mr. Blake," he said. "I just caught sight of a man I haven't seen for quite a few years. I was wondering what on earth he would be doing in Manila, and in the company of a man like his companion, I knew them both when I used to be on this coast in the Merchant Service."

Blake turned his head a trifle, and saw that the two men who had roused the captain's curiosity were Count Flambert and Lacroix.

"I think I met both of them this afternoon," he remarked, turning back. "You mean Count Flambert and the man known as Lacroix?"

Captain Vaughan looked surprised.

"I didn't know you had met them," he said.

Blake lighted a cigarette. "What do you know about them, captain?"

"Not much, but enough to know that Lacroix is a wrong 'un. I used to see him in Shanghai and Yokohama and Hong Kong. He has been working the China coast for years. I guess every captain between Calcutta and Nagasaki has had him as a passenger, or as one of the crew, at some time or other. Sometimes he was flush— very flush— and at others he was down to sole leather."

"I sized him up exactly as that type," remarked Blake. "But about the other—the count?"

Captain Vaughan scratched his chin reflectively.

"I am a little hazy about him," he said slowly, after a few minutes. "I used to know him in Saigon. He was planting in a big way there when I was on the coast. We used to have his produce in our cargoes very often. Then, if I recollect rightly, he left Saigon.

"There was some talk about it at the time, but I can't remember what it was. I heard about him after that at Singapore and Batavia, and once in Colombo. He seems to have been knocking about the East doing nothing in particular. I have a vague idea that he was supposed to have become a 'hophead' (confirmed opium smoker), but I don't believe there was any truth in that."

"He certainly doesn't bear the marks of it now," remarked Blake.

Just then Yvonne, Tinker, Betty Barclay, and Mademoiselle Flambert came up the steps, accompanied by a couple of young naval officers. Barclay had disappeared, and Count Flambert and Lacroix had returned to the bar.

Yvonne gave Captain Vaughan the note for Anna, and the skipper, who had a sailor waiting outside the hotel, sent him off hot foot to bring the things back in the launch They sat talking, until about three-quarters of an hour later the luggage arrived, then the party broke up.

Blake and Tinker went up to their rooms to bathe and change. Blake was the first to reappear, and, as he strolled along the now almost deserted veranda, looking for a "boy" to bring him a cocktail, he saw a white figure sitting alone in one corner. As he approached nearer he heard Captain Vaughan calling to him in a low tone.

"I thought it was you," he said, as Blake went across; "but I waited to make sure. What do you think happened just after you all went up to change?" he went on.

"What was it, captain?"

"Lacroix saw me sitting here, and came across. He recognised me at once. I talked to him a little, for I was curious to know what his game can be here, particularly when I see him on friendly terms with people like you and Mr. Barclay. I thought he might be trying to put something across the millionaire, but I fancy Barclay is shrewd enough to look after himself.

"But the only thing that seemed to interest him was you, Mr. Blake. He asked me if I knew you—if I knew when you had arrived, and how long you were going to stay. He also seemed curious about my being skipper of the yacht out in the harbour; but it was the subject of you that he came back to."

"What did you tell him?"

"I told him I knew you slightly, but nothing more. I didn't let on that you were on the yacht, although he must find it out by to-morrow."

"It doesn't matter," remarked Blake. "But I can't imagine why he should be interested in me, unless he is suffering from a guilty conscience, and unless anyone of my profession makes him nervous.

"He says he only arrived in Manila this morning? He couldn't have come by the Pacific mail-boat that brought the Flamberts up from Singapore. What other steamer came in to-day, captain?"

"A Dutch boat got in this morning. She came up from Batavia."

"Then he must have come by that. Do you think, captain, you could find out just when the Dutch boat left Batavia, and when the Pacific Mail steamer left Singapore? I am rather curious to know."

"That will be easy enough, Mr. Blake. I am giving a little dinner on the yacht tonight while you are all ashore. The captain and first-officer of the Pacific Mail boat are coming, and a couple of agents from the town. I can get the exact dates."

"Thanks if you will. And now, let us go along to the bar and find a cocktail. I also am acting as host at a dinner-party this evening, and I expect my guests will begin to gather soon."

The Unwelcome Guest—And the Unwilling Eavesdropper—Count Flambert's Crime

BLAKE had arranged what he thought would prove a jolly dinner-party that night.

As he intended to do little dancing himself, he thought it would serve if he met his social obligations in that way instead. He had had a large table arranged at one end of the dining-room, and had placed Yvonne at the bottom of the table as hostess. There were, as well as the Barclays, Count Flambert and his daughter, the two young American naval officers, who had struck up a strong friendship with Tinker, Graves, and, of course, Yvonne.

This was the party as Blake had arranged it, but, before they had sat down, there had been laid still another place, much to Blake's annoyance.

Just before going in Count Flambert had approached Blake, and had asked, as a favour, that Lacroix might be included among the guests. Blake was too courteous to refuse, but it had upset his arrangement of the table to begin with, and had needed a quiet shuffling of cards after, as he found that, in some way, Lacroix had been placed by the Number One boy between Mademoiselle Flambert and Yvonne—a place he had already marked for Tinker.

He had finally indicated the seat on the other side of Yvonne and next to Graves to his unwelcome guest, and, from the occasional meaning glance that Yvonne shot at him from time to time, Blake knew that Lacroix was as unwelcome to Yvonne as to himself. He had intended placing Stephen Barclay on his right and Count Flambert next to Yvonne, but now he had them both beside him.

The younger element paid no attention to Lacroix whatsoever, being thoroughly hungry, and possessed apparently of a dozen jokes among themselves, which only they seemed to understand. Blake felt more relieved as he saw that Tinker and the two young naval officers were carrying things along with a swing, and he could see that Graves was, for him, making quite an effort to engage Lacroix in conversation.

Blake himself was, naturally, occupied more or less with his own two neighbours; but Count Flambert did not appear to be in the mood for talking, while Stephen Barclay was enjoying the light-hearted chatter of the youngsters.

About half-way through the meal, Blake, who was missing nothing, noticed that Lacroix was emptying his glass of wine much more frequently than was good form, and, later, when he called the "boy," and demanded a whisky-and-soda, Blake felt a dull anger surge up in him.

He caught the eye of the Number One boy, and spoke a few curt words to him. Lacroix looked up at the same instant, and seemed to sense that his host was countermanding his order. At any rate, the drink was not brought, and Lacroix did not repeat his request.

From time to time Blake saw Lacroix look down towards Flambert, then his gaze would fall upon the daughter, Honore Flambert, in a way that finally attracted Tinker's attention. Tinker laid down his fork, and coolly stared the other out of countenance; and, following that, Blake shot a glance at Tinker that was sufficient to tell the lad to keep his attention ready for Lacroix.

Blake felt a sense of relief when they rose to go out on the veranda for coffee.

Yvonne managed to reach his side, and, taking his arm, whispered:

"Who is he? I could see you were annoyed. Who introduced him?"

"Flambert," answered Blake. "I will tell you about it later."

Yvonne nodded and flitted away, and shortly after there was a general move to go up to the roof garden, where the weekly dance was to take place.

Blake accompanied them, and remained until they had secured tables near the floor; then, as the dancing began, he lighted a cigar, and made his way towards the lift. He intended to go down to the veranda, and smoke there quietly for a little.

He signalled his intention to Yvonne, and, as he made his way between the tables, he saw Lacroix and Count Flambert seated alone at a small table on the side. Lacroix was drinking the whisky-and-soda which he had failed to get at dinner, and the count appeared to have a glass of absinthe before him. They did not see Blake as he passed, and the latter avoided any movement that would attract their attention. He was deeply puzzled over the way in which Lacroix seemed to dominate the count, but he had no wish to solve the riddle by joining him while Lacroix was there.

On reaching the veranda, Blake ordered another coffee. He seated himself near the edge, and gazed out at the dense garden in front of the hotel, where myriads of fireflies were flitting about.

From the bushes came the heavy scent of roses and hibiscus. Far away against the black bulk of the hills the lights of the town were clustered, and overhead the velvety, tropical sky was densely sprinkled with stardust. Out in the bay could be seen the occasional light of a ship lying at anchor, and now and then the vivid flash of the searchlight on the Fleur-de-Lys would stab through the night.

Blake sat quietly enjoying it for nearly half an hour, when figures came through a door far up the veranda.

In the moment during which the light fell on them Blake recognised Count Flambert and Lacroix.

Up to now Blake had had the veranda all to himself, as everyone else had gone up to the roof-garden to watch the dancing. He had no desire to talk to either the count or his companion; then, as they began walking towards him, Blake slipped out of his chair, and, stepping off the edge of the veranda, moved a few feet to one side, until his figure was concealed by the thick bushes near at hand. He dropped the end of his cigar into the grass, and stepped on it.

It was his intention to wait there until Flambert and Lacroix had passed on to the bar, and then to make his way back to the roof-garden. But, to his chagrin, the voices broke off as the two reached the table where Blake had been sitting. Then he heard Lacroix say in thick tones:

"This will do. We can talk here. There isn't anybody about. I have something to say, and you are going to listen!"

Now, Blake had no desire to be an eavesdropper, and had Lacroix's words been of a less threatening nature he would have coughed and made his presence known. But in the tones of the adventurer, now thick with drink, he had read a threat to Flambert—a threat which the latter was, apparently, powerless to repel. It was that which decided Sexton Blake to remain where he was and listen to what Lacroix might have to say.

Little did he dream what a revelation was to be unfolded during the next few minutes.

The low murmur of Lacroix's voice continued for about ten minutes. An occasional remark was interjected by the count, but for the most part the other held the platform, and, although he was not so much under the influence of drink as to speak loudly, every syllable he uttered penetrated to Blake's hearing.

At last he broke off, and gave a harsh, triumphant laugh.

"Those are my terms, count," he said, "and I shall not vary them one iota. I am sick of chasing you up and down the China coast! I want to settle down, and you are going to provide the means for me to do it. We will complete our arrangements tomorrow morning. And now I am going up to take my future wife, Mademoiselle Honore, away from those young apes. It is with me she should be dancing!"

Blake heard the scrape of a chair, and, peering out from behind the bush that sheltered him, he saw Lacroix go swaggering up the veranda. A moment later Blake heard a deep sigh as the count rose and stumbled along towards the steps. Blake slipped out from his place of concealment, and strode over the springy turf, reaching the count just as the latter arrived at the foot of the steps. Blake laid his hand on the other's arm.

"Let us go for a short stroll across the links, count," he said quietly. "I think you may have something to tell me, and I certainly have something to say to you."

The count drew back with a sharp cry as he peered through the gloom at Blake.

"Why, I don't know what you mean, Mr. Blake!" he stammered.

"I think you will, count, when I tell you that I have just heard every word that passed between you and Lacroix."

"Oh, my heavens!" gasped the other.

"Wait!" said Blake quickly. "Don't let us discuss matters here. Come along! On the links we shall not be overheard."

The count allowed Blake to lead the way through the garden and out on to the open ground that stretched to the links. But not until a good hundred yards lay between them and the hotel did Blake speak again.

"I said I had overheard everything that passed between you and Lacroix," he repeated. "That is true, count. Believe me, I have no wish to pry into your private affairs, but, if you will permit me to say so, you seem to be in a position from which you are unable to extricate yourself. Tell me, how long has Lacroix been blackmailing you?"

"For three years," whispered the other, glancing nervously over his shoulder.

"I take it he has received a good deal of money from you in that time?"

"Most of my fortune."

"And now he desires to make a last stroke, which will strip you of what remains, and bring to him your daughter as wife. Is that right?"

"Yes."

"And do you propose yielding to the preposterous demands of this blackmailer?"

"What else can I do? If I refuse, he will notify the French authorities in Saigon that it was I—I—"

"That it was you who shot and killed a man in Saigon," put in Blake. "I gathered that much from what Lacroix said to-night. Tell me, count, did you do this thing?"

"I don't know, Mr. Blake. I wish to Heaven I did know! It seems that I did. They tell me so, and the weapon was found in my hand."

"I don't quite follow you," remarked Blake in a puzzled tone. "You say you do not know. Yet you think you must have done it. Do you mind telling me as much as you know of the affair? Believe me, I shall receive what you tell me in confidence, and it may be that I can help you."

The count stood for some time in silence, deep in thought.

As Lacroix's hand fumbled at his hip pocket, Sexton Blake's fist shot out. The adventurer went down on the grass like a pole-axed bullock. (*Chapter* 4.)

THE FOURTH CHAPTER.

Confidences—Lacroix is Impertinent, Indoors and Out—The Result—A Slight Clue

"MR. BLAKE, I will confide in you," he said, "and if you can help me, you will not only save my reason but you will also save my daughter from the disgrace of my exposure, and the infamy of being the wife of a man like Lacroix.

"Three years or more ago I was planting outside Saigon. I had a large estate and was doing well. My wife had been dead for many years, and at that time my daughter was at school in France. To my shame I confess that, occasionally, when I came into Saigon I would go to a certain villa at the edge of the native quarter and smoke opium. You know the practice is very common there.

"One night I went there, and smoked perhaps six, perhaps seven 'pipes.' How long I slept afterwards I do not know; but I awoke to find myself being shaken by the half-caste, who runs the place. As my mind cleared, I found that something was wrong. Beside him stood this man Lacroix. Across from me was another man sprawled out in one of the mat beds.

"I finally gathered that this man was dead—had been shot while he lay there. Then they told me that I had been found with the revolver in my hand, and that it was I who had killed him.

"Why should I have killed him? I had never seen him before, and I had nothing against him. Nor had I seen Lacroix before. But both he and the half-caste said they had heard the shot, and had rushed in to find me dropping back on the bed with the pistol in my hand. They said I must have done it during some frenzied dream.

"I could not deny it, for I did not know anything about it. Then they said if I got away at once they would get rid of the body and hush the thing up. Instead of facing it and trying to clear it up I yielded. I was in a panic of fear when I thought what the disgrace would mean to my daughter, who was even then on her way to Saigon. So I did as they said.

"Since then I have been at the mercy of Lacroix. The blackmailing began about a month afterwards, and just when my daughter had arrived. I was forced to meet his demands, and these were repeated at short intervals. At last I saw that my fortune was going, and that if that sort of thing kept up, I should be beggared. So I sold my plantation, and took my daughter to Hong Kong.

"Lacroix followed us there, and I was forced to give him more money. Then followed flights to Singapore, Colombo, Batavia and, finally, we came here to Manila. Sometimes for months we would be left alone; then Lacroix would appear on the scene, and we would have to steal away again.

"To-night he has made, what he says is his last demand. He insists that I pay him one hundred thousand China dollars, and give my dear daughter to him in marriage. It means ruin and disgrace! I would take the easy way out and make a quick end of it all, but I dare not leave Honore alone in the world at the mercy of a man such as he is. That is all, Mr. Blake."

Blake had listened closely to all the count had to say. Now he asked one question.

"Tell me, count," he said. "when you went to the villa that night, did you have a revolver with you?"

"No. I had no weapon of any sort. I don't know where the pistol came from that was found in my hand."

"It looks as though you had been the victim of a plant," went on Blake. "But of course it doesn't do you much good unless we can prove that, I think—"

Blake broke off as the other grasped his arm convulsively and pointed to a dark figure that was swinging towards them.

"Lacroix," he gasped.

"Here, man, pull yourself together," commanded Blake sharply. "If it is Lacroix leave him to me."

They stood watching whilst the blurred figure grew more distinct. It soon became evident that Lacroix was suffering from strong emotion, for his arms were flailing about and he was muttering to himself.

Finally, as he saw them, he broke off and came on at what was almost a run. He drew up in front of them, panting heavily.

"You—you!" he snarled at the count, "I want you to come back to the hotel at once. That little vixen of a daughter of yours has just slapped my face in front of everyone."

At this point he suddenly seemed to become aware of Blake's presence, "Yes, and that confounded cub who travels with you helped to put me out of the roof garden," he cried, glaring at Blake.

Blake stood with his thumbs thrust into the tops of his evening trousers under the dip of his white mess jacket.

"I should say that the young man you refer to as a 'cub' showed good sense," he drawled. "M. Lacroix, take my advice and go to bed. You have had too much to drink."

"I go to bed when I choose, and I don't take suggestions from you, Mr. Blake," rasped the other.

All the same he appeared to make an attempt to pull himself together, and, in doing so, realised that it was Sexton Blake who was standing out on the links alone with the count. The thing had, to Lacroix's mind, all the marks of secrecy about it. He peered suspiciously at the count.

"What are you doing here?" he asked thickly.

Blake stepped quietly between the two men. "M. Lacroix, you are very impertinent. I have already told you that you have had too much to drink. If you do not wish to go to bed, you may go to the dickens. But you will at least leave us."

"Curse you! I'll—"

"You will do nothing," broke in Blake evenly. "But, unless you leave us at once, you will find that I shall do something. Are you going?"

"I am going, and Count Flambert is coming with me!"

"You are going, and Count Flambert remains with me."

"No!" almost shouted Lacroix, who was beside himself with anger and suspicion.

Blake took a step forward. "Put up your hands, M. Lacroix," he snapped. "I am going to knock you sober."

Instead of putting up his hands, Lacroix half crouched, and his hand went towards his hip. Blake waited no longer but bent forward a little. The next instant, even as Lacroix's hand fumbled at his pocket, Blake's right shot out. It caught Lacroix on the point of the jaw, and he went down like a pole-axed bullock.

"I am afraid I did that rather deliberately," remarked Blake as he bent over the prone figure of the adventurer. "But I particularly wanted this," and he held up the heavy automatic which he had taken from Lacroix's hip pocket.

He got to his feet, and held the weapon out to the count.

"You can't examine it very closely by starlight," he remarked, "but tell me, count, is this weapon anything like the one that was found in your hand that night in the villa."

The count took the pistol and held it close to his eyes. He turned it over and over in his hands, then handed it back.

"It was the same type of weapon," he replied. "The one found in my hand was .38 calibre, but I do not know the make."

"This is also a .38," said Blake as he slipped it into his pocket. "Now listen to me, count. I want you to drop your fear of this blackmailer. When he comes round he will realise that he has made a bad blunder this evening. He already suspects that you may have told me something about your affairs. In that case he will try to terrify you into immediate acquiescence.

"We don't know what happened on the roof garden, but I gather that he must have insisted on dancing with your daughter and that she refused him. Then, under the influence of drink, he probably became offensive, and, in her anger, she slapped his face.

"That would be enough for Tinker, and I think we shall find that Tinker and his friends, the young naval officers, put Lacroix out of the place by force.

"But your surrender to this man and fear of exposure must stop. I want you to place yourself in my hands, and allow me to deal with Lacroix. I have a plan in my mind; but before deciding definitely it will be necessary for me to consult with Mademoiselle Cartier, as I am her guest.

"In the meantime, I want to get into Lacroix's room at the hotel before he returns. Do you know where it is?"

"Yes. I walked that far with him before dinner when he went up to change."

"Then come on, count. We have no time to lose."

With that Blake turned and started back across the links, the count nervously shambling along at his side.

The Arrival at Saigon—Discussing Plans —Blake Surmises —And Prepares for Action.

JUST four days later a beautiful, snow-white yacht steamed slowly up the Saigon River, and docked at one of the river piers belonging to a French shipping line.

Although Captain Vaughan, of the Fleur-de-Lys, knew every bend and shallow in the channel, the yacht had taken on a pilot at the mouth of the river, for in the East the river-pilots— "mudpilots," they call them there—are very strict in observing their privileges, and, being an experienced mariner who knew all the ropes, Captain Vaughan was not the man to rouse their animosity.

He acted on the theory that there might come a time when he would need a pilot urgently, and he preferred to keep on such terms with them that should such an occasion arise, there would be no fear of mysterious delays.

It had been a good many years since a private yacht as large as the Fleur-de-Lys had come to Saigon, and that in itself was sufficient to create a lively curiosity among the dock-side natives; while her name inspired an added interest among the French Colonials who viewed her from their office windows.

The press of eager natives grew denser and denser on the dock while the medical and Customs formalities tended to, and when the gangway was finally lowered over the side Captain Vaughan had to station a quartermaster at the top to prevent them from swarming on board.

On the after-deck, under the double awning which had been raised, sat the owner and a group of her guests. In addition to those who had originally sailed from London, there had been added at Manila, Stephen Barclay and his daughter, and Count Flambert and his daughter.

With the exception of Yvonne and Tinker, all the others had been considerably surprised at the decision to leave Manila in the early hours of the morning following the dance on the roof-garden of the Manila Hotel.

And there were at least two doleful young men who careened madly round and round the yacht as she slipped out of the bay, waving their hands, and shouting until the screws churned up the water as the yacht went full speed ahead. They were two young naval officers, who looked upon the departure as a sad tragedy.

There was also a third person left in Manila who awoke that day to find the hotel veranda strangely deserted by those in whom he was particularly interested, but who succeeded in finding an explanation of the mystery when he found that the white yacht was no longer at her moorings.

That person was Lacroix.

After his consultation with Yvonne, Sexton Blake had acted swiftly. He had spent a surreptitious half-hour in Lacroix's room, going shamelessly and methodically through that gentleman's luggage. When Blake had emerged he had carried with him a small bundle, which he carefully deposited in his own room.

Then he had sought Stephen Barclay, and had communicated sufficient to that gentleman to explain their reasons for leaving Manila at such short notice. As the millionaire was simply idling about the East, a change of arrangements did not affect his plans, and he was pleased to accept Yvonne's invitation for him and Betty to accompany them to Saigon.

Blake had had a struggle to overcome the count's fear of Lacroix. He had been under the thumb of the latter for so long, and the threat of disgrace had assumed such proportions in his mind, that he was in a state of nerves that forbade any attempt at cool or collected thinking.

Sexton Blake, on the other hand, was not handicapped in this way, and, while he realised that he might be mistaken, he was prepared to wager a substantial sum that Lacroix would not carry out his threat, at least, for the present. And before any exposure he could make would be effective, Blake was determined to dig up the truth of just what happened that night in the Saigon villa.

As for Mademoiselle Honore, she was only too delighted to get away from any place where she must be brought into contact with Lacroix.

They were now discussing their plans for the day. It was nearly lunch-time when they docked, so it was decided that they should have tiffin on the yacht; then, later in the afternoon, when it was cool, most of them would go ashore. Count Flambert was to remain on board with Blake, but Honore was to go with the others. Graves, too, elected to remain on board. Tinker, after he had received explicit directions from Blake, which were based on information supplied by the count, was to go on a private scouting expedition, and return to the yacht to report.

Blake knew that he himself could not make a definite move before nightfall, and, in view of the plan he had in mind, he thought it wiser that he should not be seen. He knew, moreover, that he might not have very much time in which to work before Lacroix would appear in Saigon. They had given him the slip successfully enough in Manila, but Blake realised it was only a matter of a few hours before the adventurer would find out that the yacht had cleared for Saigon.

He might have to go to Hong Kong by the Pacific mail-boat, and get a French steamer there for Saigon; but, on the other hand, he might pick up something in Manila which was bound for the coast of French Indo-China —either Haiphong or Saigon. At any rate, it was a certainty that Lacroix would strain every effort to overtake them.

While Blake felt positive that the affair at the villa had been a deliberate plant, with Count Flambert as the victim, he knew it was going to be no easy matter to prove this. And without that proof the count was at the mercy of the treacherous tongue of the adventurer.

The affair could not stand analysis under the cold light of reason. In half a dozen places Blake could tear to pieces the fabric which Lacroix had woven about the drug soddened count that night. Had the count been in a normal state, and had he stoutly maintained his innocence, threatening to fight the thing to a finish, Blake was certain the crime never would have been fastened on to him.

But he had yielded. He had paid blackmail for more than three years. It was too late now to come out and protest innocence without overwhelming proof. The first question the French Commissaire of Police would ask would be:

"If you are innocent of this crime, M. le Count, then why have you paid blackmail all this time? Why did you not seek our protection before, and leave it to us to uncover the guilty person?"

And now the count was not in a position to face that question. Thus Blake reasoned, even though at the time he smiled inwardly at the thought that of his own volition he had plunged into a case when he vowed that nothing should tempt him to do so while he was on holiday.

He was seated under the fan in the main saloon when Tinker returned. Graves and Count Flambert were aft under the awning having tea, and, since the others had not returned, Blake and Tinker had the saloon to themselves.

"Well, my lad," said Blake, "what about it?"

"The place is still in existence, guv'nor," answered Tinker, "but I am afraid I didn't discover much else, except that the half-caste described by the count seems still to be running it."

"How did you ascertain that?"

"I went as far as the Hotel de l'Europe with the others," explained Tinker. "I got an old carriage there, and, on the pretence that I just wanted to see the place, told the man to drive through the suburbs. I soon recognised the road, because it was the same that you and I passed along several times on our last visit here.

"As soon as I spotted the groves which the count had described I stopped the carriage, and paid off the man. I then poked about a bit, but managed all the time to work my way nearer the quarter where the villa stands.

"There is an old Buddhist temple in the grove there, and as there were a few French tourists visiting it, my presence did not excite any curiosity. Well, sir, I finally struck the lane of which we were told, and, going by the count's directions, I soon spotted the house. I can imagine it is pretty weird place at night, guv'nor, for it gives one the creeps even in daylight. It just felt as if there was something wrong about the spot, if you gather what I mean, sir."

"I understand what you mean, Tinker. Proceed."

"Of course, I knew it was quite possible that I was being watched from half a dozen different spots, but I fooled about, picking flowers here and there, and taking an occasional snapshot of the grove with the little vest-pocket Kodak I took along with me. In this way I worked my way to the back of the villa; but I couldn't see much there.

"As in front, it was shut off by a high bamboo fence. I got close to the fence, and tried to look through. At last I found a place where I could just glimpse the inside. It seemed nothing but a tangled jungle of bushes and grass and flowers, with a bit of the back veranda of the house. I couldn't see a soul.

"I was just going to give it up, for I knew it was too risky to stay there much longer, when I heard a sound on the other side of the fence. I stayed where I was, and a few seconds later I saw a half-caste walk along to the end of the veranda. I hadn't noticed it before, but now I saw a birdcage there, with a mynah-bird in it. The Eurasian talked to it for some time, and while he did I studied him. But one look was enough to show me that he was the same man described by the count.

"He had a perfectly bald head, very large, and hung forward. His eyes were Chinese all right, but his nose and mouth were European enough. His body was bent and twisted, and his arms were as long as those of an orang-utang. I knew it was the same, and I also knew the opium joint must still be in existence.

"After that I thought I had better make tracks, so I did. I came straight back here to report."

"You have discovered more than I had hoped," remarked Blake. "You have established the two facts which are essential to my plans."

"I say, guv'nor, if I may digress, why is it that people like that Eurasian have such a fancy for birds? I have never been able to puzzle it out."

"Nor anyone else," answered Blake. "And yet it is a fact that in a very large percentage of cases the worst classes of criminals have a weakness for birds. And this fancy is strongest among those who are the slyest and most cunning of all. I remember Cranowitz, a dangerous German we ran to earth in a London suburb during the war (you will recall the case, Tinker), had an extensive aviary in his back garden. It is an odd psychological twist that has never been explained. But it has become so well established among criminal investigators that it is now a common saying among them: 'Show me a man who keeps birds and I will show you a wrong 'un.' Of course that's an exaggeration—lots of very respectable people keep birds.

"But to return to the business in hand. I shall go ashore just after dusk. I have already laid out the clothes which I took from Lacroix's room in Manila. Of course, there is always the danger that he may have cabled to the Eurasian, if, as must be the case if my theory is to hold water, they are accomplices.

"But I must risk that. A solution of the mystery can only be found in the villa where the crime occurred. When I have had a look round there, then something may occur to me."

"In both senses of the word!" chipped in Tinker. "Surely you are not going alone, guv'nor? Even if I don't go inside, I ought to be on guard outside."

Blake shook his head. "Not this time, my son! This is only a preliminary visit, and I fancy it will be necessary for me to go again.

If so, I shall not be able to go disguised as Lacroix. That will never serve for more than one night, and it may not serve even for that time. I can't tell what will happen until I get inside the place. But the next time there will be plenty for you to do."

And with that Tinker had to be content,

Even as Blake stood hesitating for an instant, several yellow figures hurled themselves out of the surrounding shrubbery upon him, and he found himself struggling and crashing among the bushes, fighting madly against his unknown foes. (*Chapter* 6.)

THE SIXTH CHAPTER.

In Disguise —Passing the Test —The Mysterious Warning —Why? —No Retreat —The Opium Joint —Ambushed.

AFTER dark that evening a tall, spare figure descended the gangway of the yacht and walked leisurely up the dock.

Count Flambert, who had been called in to criticise, had declared that even he himself could hardly tell the difference between the man before him and Lacroix,

Blake had donned a black-striped white flannel suit of the kind affected most by Lacroix. As they were of about the same build, the fit was excellent. Lacroix, being clean-shaven like Blake, it was not easy to bring the features to the point of similarity which he desired, but he was assisted a good deal by the fact that Lacroix's nose and chin were of the same type as his. He had worked away patiently at the deeper lines of the face until he had at last achieved the effect he was after, and when, with a soft Panama hat of Lacroix's pulled well down over his eyes in exactly the same way in which Lacroix had worn it, he had come out on deck, Yvonne had pronounced the disguise perfect.

And Sexton Blake knew it would have to be good enough to pass the penetrating gaze of the half-caste if he were to gain access to the opium "joint" that night. But it was no part of his calculations that his disguise might be penetrated even before he reached the villa.

Blake was determined that his initial inquiries should be made alone. He would not consent to Tinker accompanying him even part of the way. It was just after dusk when the little group on deck watched him disappear down the gangway. They caught a glimpse of him as he made his way along the short wharf, then he became lost in the shadows of the riverside godowns; and two of the watchers turned back with an expression of worry showing in their eyes.

It was Blake's intention to make first for the Hotel de l'Europe and secure some sort of vehicle there which would take him through the European suburb to the native compound which was his objective. The veranda terrace was crowded when he arrived, but there was a small table at one end where he sat down. He decided that it was as yet a little early for his proposed exhibition, so, ordering an iced drink, he sat watching the crowds.

He had been there for about ten minutes or so when he suddenly became aware that a man at a nearby table was regarding him with surreptitious interest. For a moment Blake forgot his role, and tried to recall it he had ever seen the man before. Then he remembered that the other might have known Lacroix at some time.

With his mind occupied over this, Blake paid no attention to the fact that the Tongkinese "boy," who was serving him, was taking a much longer time over pouring out his drink and stirring the contents than was necessary. He was standing just beside Blake's right elbow, and Blake could not see that the boy's slant eyes were studying him beneath lowered lids.

Nor did he dream for a single moment that a few minutes later a coolie was speeding out towards the villa in the native compound with a message for the half-caste keeper of the opium joint.

A few minutes later the man who had shown a surreptitious interest in Blake got up from his table and strolled casually across to where the detective sat. He nodded, and, drawing out a chair, sat down. Blake returned the nod, but the newcomer did not speak until the boy had departed. Then he leant forward, and, with his lips scarcely moving, said:

"You have some nerve to come back to Saigon, Lacroix. Or don't you know what everyone else on the coast knows?"

Blake gave a defiant grunt.

"Why shouldn't I come back to Saigon?" he asked in low tones that matched the other's.

The stranger looked at him in amazement.

"Where have you been for the past year? Haven't you heard what Honan Pierre says?"

"No. What does he say?"

The other turned and took a careful look about him; then he bent forward again.

"He says you double-crossed him, and that he wants to see you— just once. You ought to know what that means. I am giving you the tip, because I don't like to see a man walk into any devil's trap that Honan Pierre might spring.

"Besides, I don't forget the little favour you did for me in Haiphong. And one thing more. Lacroix, before I go—the Annamese girl, Kulai Tui, whom you smuggled along when you came from

Haiphong with Journet is out at Honan Pierre's place. That's all. Take my tip and get away from Saigon."

With that Blake's strange informant rose, and, although Blake made a quick gesture for him to remain, he shook his head. A few moments later he had disappeared in the throngs which were passing along the street.

Blake was puzzled. It was plain enough that the man who had warned him had taken him for Lacroix. To that extent his disguise had stood the test. Who the man might be, Blake, of course, had not the remotest idea. By his cut there could be little doubt that he belonged to the same army of coast adventurers to which Lacroix belonged, and apparently Lacroix had done the other a favour of some sort in Haiphong.

But who was Honan Pierre? And what rumour was there in the underworld of the coast that said Lacroix was in danger from this person? Again, who was the Annamese girl, Kulai Tui, whom Lacroix had apparently smuggled down to Saigon from Annam?

Was Honan Pierre the keeper of the opium joint? Was he, as Blake had suspected in Manila, a partner with Lacroix in the blackmailing of Count Flambert? In that case, how had Lacroix double-crossed the other? Had he kept back some of the money that should have been paid to Honan Pierre?

Blake knew that would be ample reason for an Eurasian opium joint keeper to declare a revenge, and he imagined it was not far from the truth.

But, whatever might be the explanation of it all, one thing now stood out clearly to Blake. It would be folly for him to attempt to enter the joint disguised as Lacroix.

Yet in that villa in the native compound in Saigon lay the secret of the crime which had been committed that night over three years before. And there, too, was hidden the key which could unlock the mystery which had made Count Flambert a man without a country and a man without home.

Blake pondered the matter for some time.

At first he had been half-inclined to go back to the yacht and endeavour to elicit further facts from the count which might throw a little more light on the warning he had received at the hotel. But, finally, he determined to go ahead with his original plan—with one variation. He would, on the way to the villa, make the few changes in his appearance which would remove all likeness to Lacroix. He would, of course, still be wearing the adventurer's clothes and hat, but the lines of pigment and grease which had altered his features would be removed.

Thus it was his intention to gain access to the joint simply as a traveller who had come to Saigon; and Blake trusted to his own knowledge of the China coast to get past any interrogatory. But he knew nothing of the message which had already been sent to Honan Pierre, nor did he know that already there were eyes in the grove watching for the coming of "Lacroix."

Blake chose an ancient fiacre in the square by the hotel, and using the code given to him by the count, directed the driver. As soon as they had left the brightly lighted streets and had entered the darker confines of the European suburb, Blake set to work, and, long before they had reached the grove, he had succeeded in removing all traces of his disguise.

And in the lane before the villa, where the carriage finally drew up, it was too dark for the driver to notice any difference in the man who descended and paid him liberally and the one who had entered the vehicle back in the square.

Blake waited until the carriage had been swallowed up in the darkness. When the sound of the wheels had died away in the soft sand of the lane, he stood listening for a few minutes more; then, cautiously feeling his way, he made for the gate, which, according to the count's directions, he should find in the high bamboo fence which shut off the grounds of the villa from the lane.

He found it without much difficulty. Raising his hand, he beat softly upon the bamboo poles, then waited. He heard a slight rustling sound, followed by a faint creak.

It was so dark that it was almost impossible for him to see what was happening, but he sensed instinctively that the gate was being unfastened. He kept his hand on it, and suddenly felt it swing inwards.

He stepped forward until he had passed within.

He heard the gate close, and stood waiting for the challenge which the count had told him would surely come.

He had also been told of the scrutiny by electric torch to which he would be subjected on reaching the veranda. Therefore, Blake was not startled as, without the slightest warning, a bright light was flashed full into his eyes. For a moment only it rested on his features, then the circle travelled down his body, taking in each detail of his dress.

As far as Blake could make out, the light seemed to come from the dense bushes on the right of the path; but before he could locate it definitely it was gone again. Still a little dazzled, Blake hesitated for a few seconds. Things had not happened quite as Count Flambert had said they would. And now, would the challenge come? Or should he risk it, and make his way up the path towards the veranda? The decision was not to be left to Blake, for even as he stood there a sharp crashing of branches sounded, and the next instant several figures hurled themselves out of the darkness upon him.

His suspicions had not had time to crystallise into a definite action of advance or retreat, and now he found himself struggling and crashing among the bushes, fighting blindly against his unknown foes.

Blake's fist got home time after time with dull thud following dull thud against an unseen body. But as quickly as he drove off the more persistent of his assailants, just as rapidly did others take their places.

Blake knew that his first efforts must be confined to reaching the gate again, if possible. The enemy seemed equally determined to drag him deeper into the jungle of bushes and creepers. They swayed back and forth, panting, snarling, and clawing at him; and, despite the terrible punishment he was handing out, he knew that he was getting the worst of it. He realised in that moment that his only hope was to make a sudden break, and try to reach the gate. Once there he might hold them off until he had succeeded in getting the bamboo gate open, and if he could only reach the lane he was willing to take his chances among the trees in the grove.

But even as Blake essayed to put this plan into execution, a new assault was launched upon him from behind.

He felt a thin, bony arm go about his throat, then he experienced a sharp stinging sensation in the shoulder as something was plunged into the flesh. He rocked dizzily for a second, then his senses reeled, and he crashed into the trampled bushes unconscious.

There followed a few low grunts, a whispered conversation in Tongkinese dialect, then the limp body of the detective was picked up, and carried through the tangled jungle of the garden.

THE SEVENTH CHAPTER.

Back to Consciousness —The Hooded Death—A Terrible Ordeal—
Saved by Self Control.

SLOWLY consciousness returned to Sexton Blake. In a vague way his mind was functioning; but so intermixed with its normal adjustment were the crazy pictures which were being projected by his subconsciousness, that it was some time before he began to find it possible to sort out the imaginary from the real. But when his conscious effort began to make itself felt his mind regained its normal plane, and Blake opened his eyes.

His most distinct impression at that moment was that his mouth was extra-ordinarily dry. His throat muscles felt half paralysed, and his head was aching with slow painful throbs that told of severely abnormal blood pressure. Blake was too experienced a student of drugs not to know that he had been the victim of a powerful opiate.

How long he had been unconscious he could not tell. But as he lay relaxed, gazing about him, his eyes became fixed on a small oblong square of light, which he finally determined was the first grey of dawn coming through a small window. It was the barest suggestion, and not sufficient to enable him to see his surroundings.

He was lying on his back with his arms stretched out straight by his sides. His feet seemed to be free enough, and slowly it came to him that, wherever he was, he was not bound.

It was this discovery which determined him to struggle to his feet, and make a tour of his prison, or whatever sort of place it was into which he had been thrown, for now he recalled the events which had occurred before he had been plunged into unconsciousness.

All this time he had been oppressed by a suffocating sensation in his chest, which he had vaguely put down as due to the increased blood pressure caused by the drug, and the subsequent exhaustion of the lungs. He thought he would find some relief if he sat up, and, with this intention, he moved his arms and lifted his head.

The next second Blake had tensed his arms, and lowered his head, as there came a sudden movement of the weight on his chest, and through the darkness there sounded a sharp hiss.

In that moment Sexton Blake knew that what had oppressed him so was no congestion of the arteries, or exhaustion of the lungs, but a living menace which lay upon him.

Blake allowed his arms to relax ever so slowly, he lay scarcely breathing, trying to think what he should do.

It all became clear enough to him now, and with the danger which threatened him the last effects of the drug vanished. His mind became alert and worked swiftly, for he knew that only one thing could save him, and that was his wits.

It was easy enough now to understand why he had not been bound. It was only too evident what had happened after he had been drugged into unconsciousness. His captors had dragged him into this place, whatever it was, and had left him there at the mercy of a deadly snake.

It was a matter of sheer luck that the reptile had not struck while he slept. Blake knew that it could only have been because he lay utterly motionless under the stupefying effect of the drug. He knew of many instances where men in the East had awakened to find a snake coiled up on their chest or at their feet; and he knew, too, that it was hardly likely the creature would strike unless he made some movement.

It was the natural instinct of a snake to seek the warmth of a living body in the chill hours of the night, and Blake realised with what vicious cunning his captors had put that knowledge to their use.

It might mean hours of silent agony on the part of the man before sheer physical exhaustion forced him to move and alarm the snake. And well his captors had counted on that happening, if not during his period of unconsciousness, then on his waking. And death by snake bite in that country was no uncommon thing.

For the moment the creature seemed to have subsided. The motionless weight on his chest told Blake that it had probably sunk back into its coils. He could not see what sort of snake it was, but that it was of a large species he knew from its great weight.

He turned his eyes towards the tiny window, and found that the patch of grey had grown much lighter with the spreading dawn. Dimly he began to make out little details of the place in which he lay.

It seemed to be the inside of a small mud hut, of which the small window high up appeared to be the only means of light. He could make out the shadowy lines of the crossed bamboo, which supported the thatched roof, and, to his left, he saw what he took to be a door. But, as yet, his own body was in shadow, and he could not distinguish the coiled reptile which lay upon him.

50

He knew he must wait for more light to filter in. Not until he could discover the type of snake which menaced him could he decide what to do. If it were of a non-poisonous variety, then he knew that his only course was to pit his own strength against its coils.

But if it should be a venomous one, then what could he do? The slightest movement would disturb it, and Blake knew that when a poisonous snake is disturbed its first act is to strike.

It needed every ounce of his iron control to lie there waiting while the dawn should brighten. An occasional sliding movement of the coils on his chest told him that the snake only half slumbered. His first motion had made it restless, and it was now in that state of half-waking which is most dangerous. How those minutes dragged past is impossible of description—how the man lay there waiting, waiting, waiting, scarcely breathing, yet conscious each terrible moment of the proximity of that lightning death stroke which lay poised above him.

Only Blake ever knew the agony of that silent watch while the grey dawn lightened and crept slowly across the roughly boarded floor of the hut, until it touched the man's body, and revealed to sight the awful thing that menaced him.

He first made out a veritable mountain which lay heaped upon him, then beneath lowered lids he followed the revelation of twisted, glistening coils, until, with a great leap of the heart which he thought must rouse the creature, he saw, not six inches from his throat, the fat, ugly head of a hooded cobra—one of the deadliest of the poison reptiles.

And in that moment Sexton Blake knew that death was very near.

Now Blake also knew three things about the cobra. He knew, firstly, that no movement of his could by any human chance be quick enough to hurl the snake from him before it struck.

Even if this had been a possibility, it would have been able to strike before he could get to his feet, and try to circumvent it in some way. In that his chance would have been a very slim one, for there is nothing more vicious to tackle than an angered cobra.

Blake knew further that, while he lay without moving the snake might not strike. But they could not remain in this position for an indefinite time. Sooner or later snake or man must make a move, and, if the former, then Blake's life depended on its whim.

And it was in his third bit of knowledge of the cobra that lay his only hope.

On that, and that alone, could he pit his strength of control.

This was the fact that the cobra dislikes the light—either the light of day or the light of a lamp. With the spread of dawn its natural instinct would be to seek a darker spot. If this habit should prevail, then would it but seek to crawl beneath the body of the man—would the warmth of living contact make it reluctant to leave? Or would it leave him even as it had come to him? For and against—it was an even chance!

As time passed it became more and more agonising to lie tense and motionless. Time and again his burning throat contracted, and it needed every ounce of will power to control the tortured muscles which threatened to seek relief in a fit of violent coughing. He dared not even swallow for fear of rousing the cobra. And thus they lay, man and reptile, until each detail of the place became distinct, and the grey patch which was visible through the small window turned to azure.

Then the crisis came—came so suddenly that, for a moment, Blake closed his eyes and waited. Slowly, ever so slowly, the twisted coils on his chest moved. Blake could feel the slow quiver of action pass through the entire length of the cobra's body.

He lifted his lids the barest trifle, and forced himself to face the danger.

He saw the flat, ugly head raised up, and the neck arch in a curve as the cobra spread its hood and swung its head slowly from side to side. There followed a faint hiss, and then the reptile became motionless, its eyes fixed on the man's face. How long it remained thus Blake could not have told. It may have been two minutes, it may have been twenty minutes. Time did not exist for him in that awful moment.

It seemed an eternity of waiting, until at last the repulsive head turned, and the coils rippled once more. Slowly, with an awful grace, the snake thrust its head outwards, and turned from the man, its hooded head waving about over the floor.

Inch by inch, lazily with a maddening deliberation of movement, it stretched out until the front part of its body touched the floor. Then came another quivering ripple, and one great coil slowly straightened out. Another and another followed, while Blake watched with fascinated gaze. But not even when the tapering point of tail slithered over his arm and followed the sinuous course of the rest of the creature did he move. Full twelve feet of fighting death, he saw, making its way slowly across the floor. Foot by foot it crept, until in one corner where the floor boards were laid roughly Blake saw it pause.

Still Blake waited.

If it should return, he was tensed ready to spring up and tear up one of the boards as a weapon.

But it did not turn. Instead its head sought carefully what lay beneath, then, apparently satisfied that no danger lurked there, it disappeared through the opening with the same slow deliberation that had marked its every movement.

Sexton Blake drew a deep breath, and allowed his body to relax. He lay for a few moments, slowly stretching his cramped limbs and working the muscles of his thighs and arms. Then he turned over on his side and got to his feet. Keeping a wary eye on the hole through which the cobra had disappeared, Blake bent down and grasped the loose edge of one of the floor boards.

He gave a quick heave and it came away. He waited then to see if the cobra would reappear, but the snake gave no sign. Then Blake gazed down at himself.

He saw that the suit which he had been wearing the night before was covered with mud and other stains. His hat was nowhere to be seen. A brief search revealed that his pistol had been taken away, but otherwise he seemed to have been thrown into the hut just as he was.

"They felt pretty sure of the cobra getting me," he muttered, as he gazed once more towards the hole in the floor. "I suppose they expected to come this morning and find me dead. Then it would have been a simple matter to throw me into some lane, and allow me to be found. And who could ever prove it was anything else but a plain case of snake bite. But why? That is what puzzles me unless — I wonder if that is possible? Was I taken for Lacroix in the dark? And was it for him that this choice little affair was staged? If so, then there was certainly more than a little truth in the warning I received at the hotel.

"But by heavens, someone is going to pay for this! I don't know where I am, but I'll get out of here, and when I find that villa I'll get some satisfaction for this outrage or my name isn't Sexton Blake."

And with an expression of cold anger in his eyes Blake lifted the floor board and made for the door.

Blake caught the crafty Eurasian, and, gripping his neck, jerked him back on the table. "Now, you snake!" said the detective, "You are going to get a real thrashing!" (*Chapter 8.*)

A Consultation—Tinker has his own way At Honan Pierre's—The Hold-up—Blake Exacts Vengeance—and the Truth.

WHEN dawn came that same morning, a very worried little group stood on the after deck of the Fleur-de-Lys. They were Stephen Barclay, Count Flambert, Graves, Yvonne, and Tinker. Ever since three o'clock Tinker and Yvonne had been keeping watch for Blake's return, but when the first grey streaks of dawn showed over the misty river, they had decided that something must have gone a miss with Blake's plans,

It was then that Graves had been called into consultation, and it was at his suggestion that the other two men had been roused. Until now the American millionaire had had no idea why the Fleur-de-Lys had left Manila so suddenly for Saigon. But in view of the general anxiety, Tinker and Yvonne decided to take him into their confidence. When Count Flambert had consented to this, Yvonne had informed Barclay just what had occurred in Manila, and what Blake's purpose was in going on as he had the night before.

The millionaire's comment was characteristic of him.

"If this was a British or an American colony," he drawled, "I would suggest just one line of action. But it isn't, and our friends the French are a little bit touchy about foreigners interfering with their Chink colonists on this coast. If it was otherwise, I'd say collect a few of your crew, Mademoiselle, and raid the place. I guess that would open up something all right. But the only thing seems to be to report the matter to the commissaire of police, and trust to luck."

"I don't think we can do that," objected Tinker, and Yvonne nodded her agreement. "You see." went on the lad, "if we take that course, we must tell him about Count Flambert, and I know the guv'nor doesn't want to do that yet. Moreover, we don't actually know that things have gone wrong with him, and if we started the police into action we might upset some plans he has formed. At the same time, we must do something."

"Well put, my boy," rejoined Stephen Barclay. "I guess you ought to know best what line your boss would like us to take. But what do you suggest? "

"I think that I, at least, ought to go out to the place and try and find out what has happened."

"You don't mean alone?" asked Graves quickly.

"Yes, I know the lay of the land for I have already been there. It will be much easier for me to scout round alone and find out something than if several of us went."

"But that would mean danger to you," put in Yvonne. "It would not help matters if you fell into the clutches of these people."

"Well, the guv'nor is out there, somewhere, and I am going to find him," said Tinker stubbornly. "And I think my plan is the best. If I didn't show up in say three hours from the time of leaving, then you could all take whatever steps you thought best."

They argued for some time longer, but finally Tinker won his point. It was agreed that he should go out to the villa alone, but if he had not returned to the yacht, or sent some word in two hours from the time of leaving, Yvonne was to take further action. Beyond the time limit of two hours she would not go, so Tinker had to be content.

He drank a hasty cup of coffee, and with his automatic in the side pocket of his coat, he made his way down the gangway. They saw him wave his hand just before he reached the road, then he disappeared round a corner.

Tinker found a carriage only a short distance from the dock, and, after a considerable amount of prodding, managed to wake the dirty native driver. He had no intention of being driven the whole way to the lane where the villa stood, for he knew that, even at that early hour, the carriage would probably attract attention.

When Tinker came in sight of the grove which was his landmark, he gave the native another prod, and that worthy showed much greater alacrity in stopping than he had in starting; even though Tinker rewarded him with double fare.

Tinker sprang from the low vehicle and walked slowly along until the carriage had rattled back along the road he had just come. Then he quickened his footsteps and cut across towards the grove.

Tinker's plan was very different from that which he had pursued on his previous visit to the villa. Instead of a surreptitious reconnoitring, he had decided on open tactics, and with this in view he strode boldly down the lane, although his right hand was thrust loosely into the pocket of his khaki jacket, and his fingers curled lightly about the butt of the automatic which lay there.

When he arrived at the enormous banyan tree that he knew stood just opposite the gate, he turned and made for the high bamboo fence.

The gate looked rickety enough by day, but Tinker knew well that its appearance was cunningly deceptive. He rattled it loudly, and stood waiting, every sense on the "qui vive."

To his first summons there came no answer, nor could he hear any sounds within. He applied his feet to the gate the second time, and kept up a hearty tattoo, until, after some minutes, he heard a voice on other side of the gate.

He desisted and waited. Again the voice came, and Tinker recognised the low French patois of the Saigon Eurasian.

"What is it, and what do you want?" the voice demanded.

Tinker replied in the patois, stating that he wanted admission, and wanted it at once.

There was a brief silence, then the gate lurched inwards, and Tinker slipped through quickly. He turned sharply, and found himself confronting the same Eurasian whom he had seen on his former visit.

He knew him by now as the same man to whom Count Flambert had referred.

Tinker wasted no time in beating about the bush. He was convinced that Blake had come to that place the night before, and he had a shrewd suspicion that he had not yet left it. Whether his stay might be of his own volition or not Tinker didn't know, but he was determined to find out.

"You had a visitor here last night," he said curtly in the patois. "He came here to smoke opium. He was a tall man, dressed in a white suit with black stripes. He wore a wide Panama hat. I want to see him!"

The Eurasian gazed at him without blinking.

"I do not know what you mean, young master," he said evenly. "You have come to the wrong place. There is no opium here. No man came here last night. This is only private place, and I am poor man. What should I know about strange man?"

"You lie, you half-caste dog, and you know it!" snarled Tinker. "That game doesn't go with me! I know this is an opium house, and plenty of other people know it. My friend came here last night. I want him, and I want him quick! Hurry up, or by thunder, you dog, I'll give you the worst beating you ever had in your life!"

The half-caste spread out his long ape-like arms. In the early morning light he had a ghastly yellow colour that filled Tinker with loathing. His eyes looked evil enough, and Tinker knew he was at that moment on very dangerous ground.

"I tell you I not knowing what you mean!" protested the Eurasian again. "This is quite private place. You go out, and not make more trouble!"

"So that's how it is, is it?" rasped Tinker. "Then, how about this, you river rat?"

As he spoke, Tinker sprang forward, and snatched something which was clinging to a bush just beside the half-caste. The next instant he had straightened up, and, jerking his automatic, jammed the barrel into the other's ribs, while with his left hand he held before the Eurasian's eyes a tiny strip of white flannel, which showed on one side a bit of black stripe.

"You don't know anything about my friend, don't you?" he went on savagely. "You don't know anything about this piece of cloth, either, I suppose? And you don't recognise it as a piece torn from the suit he wore? Now, you 'bout turn, you dog, and lead the way to the house! If you make one move to play any monkey-tricks, you ape, I'll let a little lead into you! March!"

Tinker stepped back, and started the half-caste ahead with a vicious kick. Then, keeping him covered, he forced him along the path, and up to the veranda.

The half-caste was just stepping up, when suddenly there sounded a commotion at one end. Then Tinker saw him shrink back, and, as the lad started forward, there sprang into view a wild-looking figure that made Tinker stand stock-still in sheer amazement.

"Guv'nor!" he gasped.

"Right the first time, young 'un!" came the reply from the dishevelled-looking Blake. "And you are the early bird this morning all right. You have nabbed the very worm I was looking for!"

It was then that Tinker noticed for the first time that Blake had in his hand a short rawhide whip. He snapped it sharply under the nose of the Eurasian, who had cowered back, and was staring at him with a strange mixture of expressions.

It was clear that no one was more startled than he at the apparition which had suddenly appeared.

"What has happened, guv'nor?" asked Tinker quickly.

"I'll tell you later," replied Blake. "But first I am going to attend to our murderous friend here. Now, then, you carrion, inside the house—quick!"

Blake accompanied the words with a swish of the whip at Honan Pierre's legs. The man gave a cry of pain, and dived behind the curtain which hung over the door. Blake was after him like a flash, and Tinker followed. Blake caught his man in the centre of the room, and, gripping his neck, jerked him back until he had him pressed against the table.

Tinker stood watching while Blake's blazing anger vented itself.

"Now then, you snake!" snapped Blake. "You are going to get one real thrashing and perhaps two! You asked what happened, Tinker? Listen! I came here last night, as I intended. But no sooner was I inside the gate than I was set upon. How many there were I don't know, but I do know that it was at the instigation of this carrion.

"They drugged me with a hypodermic, and threw me into a small mud hut at the back of the compound here. I woke this morning to find a full-grown cobra lying on my chest.

"That was the pleasant companion they had thrust in upon me during the night, hoping that it would strike! Why, it doesn't matter now, but it is no thanks to this murderous rat! Nor does it matter that the attack was planned, I think, for someone else. That is why I am going to thrash him!"

With that Blake hurled the half-caste into one corner, and, raising his arm, brought the rawhide whip down with a vicious slash.

Once, twice, thrice he struck, and Tinker counted slowly up to ten while that curling lash twined round the now shrieking Eurasian. But Blake was merciless, and not until the fifteenth stroke did he desist and allow his victim to fall in a whining heap.

Blake stood, panting, gazing down at the other.

"That is just the first taste!" he snarled. "It is up to you, Honan Pierre, whether you get a second dose, and, if necessary, a third one! I—"

At that moment there was a crash, and both Blake and Tinker turned quickly, to see a weird figure coming through a panel in the wall. They saw a dishevelled-looking Chinese girl rushing towards them, and as she reached him Tinker shot out his hand, and gripped her arm. Her eyes were filled with terror, and she was gazing at Blake pleadingly. Blake studied her for a moment, and, as her lips opened and a torrent of words poured out, he held up his hand.

"Who are you, and what do you want?" he asked, in the Annamese dialect, which he had recognised as that used by the girl.

She pointed to the figure of the half-caste.

"I heard him cry," she said. "I came to plead for him!"

"Who are you?"

"I am Kulai-Tui. He gave me shelter when I had no place to go!"

Suddenly Blake recalled the strange warning he had received from the unknown adventurer at the Hotel de l'Europe the night before. "Are you from Hanoi?" he asked quickly.

The girl nodded.

"And you came to Saigon about three years ago!"

"Yes, master."

"You were smuggled down by Lacroix?"

Blake shot the question at her suddenly, and he knew from the expression in her eyes that she was the same girl of whom he had heard. But he was not prepared for what followed. The little pyjama-clad figure straightened up and her eyes blazed.

"I came with him," she said. "We were to be married. I did not see him after I landed here. Then he went away, and I was left alone. I have been protected by him." And she gestured towards the quivering figure of the half-caste.

"I think this is rather fortunate," marked Blake in English to Tinker. "Perhaps we can get the truth out of her."

Then he turned back to the girl.

"Listen to me," he said. "You are grateful to Honan Pierre? You would save him from punishment? But a much greater danger than that threatens him. If I give him to the French police it will mean that you will never see him again. But perhaps you can save him. Are you willing?"

At that moment Honan Pierre lifted his head, and started to say something to Kulai-Tui, but he subsided with a grunt as Blake flicked the whip towards him.

"You can answer my questions," went on Blake to the girl. "If you tell the truth you may save Honan Pierre. If you do not, then he goes to the police. You know what happened here one night three years ago?"

60

"I don't know what you mean, master," answered the girl, glancing towards the half-caste,

"Yes, you know," said Blake. "I speak of the night when Lacroix and his friend were here. I speak of a shooting in that room there." And he pointed towards the panel through which she had come. That night Lacroix's friend was killed, and Lacroix and Honan Pierre agreed that the crime should he laid at the door of an innocent man. Now I will tell you what happened.

"Lacroix did that killing. Honan Pierre saw him do it. Lacroix saw that they could put the blame on another man who had been smoking here that night. They made him believe that he had done it while under the influence of the opium. Then they agreed to keep the truth from the police if he would pay them money.

"He did so, and they got rid of the body of the murdered man. Shortly after that this man left Saigon, but Lacroix followed him. Lacroix was to continue to get money from him, and was to send part of it to Honan Pierre.

"But, once away from Saigon, Lacroix forgot about that, and kept everything for himself. He did not play square with Honan Pierre. Also, he had broken his pledge to you. Then you and Honan Pierre met, and discovered that each had a debt to pay to Lacroix. Yesterday you heard that Lacroix had returned to Saigon.

"You also heard that he was coming out here. The man who came was attacked and drugged. Later he was thrown into a hut, and a cobra was placed there with him. That death was devised for Lacroix. It was only a mistake that I was the man and not Lacroix. That is what has happened. Is it the truth?"

All the time Blake had been speaking Kulai-Tui had been gazing at him with fascinated eyes. He seemed to be reading the innermost thoughts of her mind, and her Oriental superstition was roused at the facility with which this stern-looking European seemed to do so. Almost against her will she nodded and said:

"Yes, master, that is the truth."

"All the truth?"

"Yes, master."

Blake turned towards Honan Pierre.

"You have heard," he said in the patois. "Is it the truth?"

The half-caste turned his sloe-black eyes towards Blake, then they went to the whip. At last he spoke.

"Yes, it is the truth," he said.

Blake gave a grunt of satisfaction, and threw the whip aside.

"Get up!" he snapped. "We will get all that down in writing while you are still able to tell the truth—yes, and you will sign it."

Fifteen minutes later Sexton Blake folded up Honan Pierre's confession and thrust it in his pocket.

"It is not much of a document," he said to Tinker, "but it will serve my purpose. I fancy when the commissaire has seen this he will act upon it."

"What about these people?" asked Tinker.

"They can't get away. We will find them here all right if we want them. Hallo! What's that, Tinker?"

This as there came a loud commotion outside.

They went to the door, and, thrusting a side the mat, gazed towards the gate. As they stood there the rickety structure was driven inwards, and through the opening came Barclay, Graves, Yvonne, Captain Vaughan, and two of the sailors from the yacht.

They gave a cry of relief as they saw Blake and Tinker on the veranda, and a moment later the detective and his assistant were trying to give them an account of what had happened.

It was when their anxiety had been satisfied that Yvonne drew Blake on one side, and said:

"Just before we left the yacht a small Japanese steamer docked. Captain Vaughan says that it has come through from Manila, as he saw it in harbour when we were there. Do you think—"

"Do I think Lacroix has come by it?" interrupted Blake. "I think there is every possibility of it, and, if so, I think I can arrange a very warm welcome for him. I will take steps at once in case it should prove to be the case."

With that Blake excused himself, and went back into the villa. He did not find either Honan Pierre or Kulai-Tui in the front room, but, on passing through the panel, he found them in the opium-room, where the half-caste was "cooking" a pill with a shaky hand.

On one of the mat beds lay a Tongkinese, asleep, but there were no other occupants.

Blake spent some twenty minutes talking to Honan Pierre, and when he finally emerged there was a look of grim satisfaction on his face.

As Honan Pierre fell to the floor in a whining heap, there came a crash, and a weird figure entered the room through a panel in the wall. It was a dishevelled Chinese girl. (*Chapter 8.*)

Lacroix Comes Back And Offers Fair Words—How Honan Pierre Gained His Pardon—The Unwitting Confession—The End of the Game—Conclusion.

EIGHT bells—midnight—were chiming out from the ships in the harbour that same night when a man came through the gloom of the lane which led to Honan Pierre's villa.

He walked with a certainty of direction that told of long familiarity with the district, and, on reaching the big banyan-tree just outside the gate, turned without hesitation. Treading softly, he reached the gate, and beat upon the bamboos.

Almost at once there came a sound from within, and the gate swung back. A few whispered words, and he was allowed to pass through. He strode up the path to the veranda, and, crossing it, lifted the mat which hung over the door. He rapped, then stood waiting.

From somewhere up the veranda a light suddenly flared, and the circle cast by a strong electric torch fell upon him, travelling slowly downwards from his hat to his feet. Then it went out, and a few seconds later the door was opened. The newcomer stepped inside, and, turning, faced Honan Pierre.

"Well, Pierre," he said, after a quick glance about the room, "I suppose you are surprised to see me?"

"Not surprised," answered the Eurasian slowly. "But why have you come here now? You went away with promises, Lacroix, none of which you have kept. You and I have nothing more to say to each other."

"Come, now, Pierre," said the visitor: "I can explain all that. I will give you your share, every dollar of it. I couldn't send it to you before. It was too dangerous."

"But not too dangerous for you to return when you discovered that a certain person had come back to Saigon!" returned the half-caste.

Lacroix shot out his hand and gripped the other's arm.

"So you know that, do you?" he hissed. "You know that Flambert is here! Yes, that is why I came back. And you and I must work together, Pierre. Come, where can we talk?"

"I have already told you that I have nothing to say, but if you must talk I will listen to you. Come to the back veranda; there is no one there."

Lacroix nodded, and waited while Honan Pierre opened the front door. He followed the half-caste out and along the veranda to the side of the villa. There they stepped into the compound and made their way to the back veranda.

Honan Pierre stepped up and squatted on his heels against the wall of the house. Lacroix felt his way cautiously, and followed suit.

If he had stopped to think he might have remembered that immediately on the other side of them was the opium room, and he would have been extremely interested if he could have seen the occupants of that room just then. More particularly would he have been intrigued by the actions of the man who occupied the mat bed which stood close to the wall on the other side of which he and the half-caste sat; for this person turned over as they stepped on to the veranda, and laid his ear against the wall where a thin panel had been slid back, allowing him to hear every word that was spoken outside.

But Lacroix did not know this, and therefore he could not guess that, during the next few minutes, by his own lips was he to condemn himself.

"I have already told you that I could explain," he said, in a low tone, as he squatted beside the half-caste. "It was impossible to send the money. But I have it, and I will give you your share."

"You talk well," replied the Eurasian. "But listen to me, Lacroix. Is it not true that on that night over three years ago, when you shot and killed Journet, we made a bargain?"

"Yes."

"Did I not keep my part of that bargain? Did I not bury your friend so that none knew of the affair?"

"Yes."

"And did we not make another man, he whom they call Count Flambert, believe that he had killed Journet?"

"Yes; but what has that to do with it? And don't go into those details, Pierre," added Lacroix, with a nervous movement.

"It is necessary to refer to those things to-night. Does not Count Flambert still believe that he did the killing?"

"Yes."

"And because he believed that, you and I made him pay us money so that he might escape the consequences. You gave me my share while you were here, but once you left you sent nothing. Now you return and say you can explain. You are too late. Lacroix!"

"Why do you say that? I tell you Flambert has returned to Saigon. We can make one last big strike, and I will give you a full half."

"While you take the other half and marry his daughter," sneered Pierre.

"How did you know that?" asked Lacroix, in a startled tone.

"How do I know anything?" asked the Eurasian evenly. "How do I know that you smuggled an Annamese girl down from Hanoi when you came with Journet, when even he knew nothing of it? How do I know that her name was Kulai-Tui, and that you had promised to marry her?"

"You devil!" snarled Lacroix. "I believe you have been double-crossing me! What, what do you know of Kulai-Tui?"

"What should I know of the one who has been my wife for two years?"

"Kulai-Tui—your wife!"

"Even so."

"Then she is here?"

"She is here." Lacroix was silent.

He began to feel uneasy. There was something in the half-caste's voice that filled him with a strange fear. He had come there that night feeling confident that after a few words he could smooth the ruffled feeling of the Eurasian, whom he held in contempt, and whom he had not hesitated to cheat, once he was clear of Saigon. But now he was not so sure.

And if Gaston Lacroix had only known that every word that had been uttered had been overheard by Sexton Blake and the Commissaire of Police of Saigon he would have fled that place as he would flee from the plague.

But he did not know this, and so he said:

"I confess that I haven't treated you well, Pierre and perhaps I treated Kulai-Tui badly. But that needn't affect us. Come on into the opium-room, and give me a pipe. I am shaky. We can talk in there."

"No, we cannot talk in there. There are others here to-night. But I will take you in. Come!"

With that Honan Pierre, who had baited the trap in order to secure his own immunity from the French law, rose and led the way back to the front of the house.

They passed through the front room, and Lacroix waited while the half-caste pushed back the panel which led to the opium-room. He stood peering in.

There seemed to be quite half a dozen men there that night, but all appeared to be asleep. Honan Pierre passed through, and Lacroix followed. Lacroix started towards an empty bed, while the Eurasian closed the panel. Lacroix was halfway down room, when one of the prone figures moved and turned over. Then Lacroix drew up with a startled oath as he found himself gazing into the business end of a heavy revolver, while a clear voice said:

"Put up your hands, Gaston Lacroix! I arrest you in the name of the Republic for the murder of Paul Journet!"

It was the voice of the Commissaire of Police.

Lacroix had lived too long by his wits not to know that he had walked into a trap.

With a lightning movement, his hand went inside his coat, where he carried a small automatic strapped under his arm, but before his fingers could close on the butt his wrist was grasped by powerful fingers.

He felt his arm jerked back, and as it was forced up between his shoulder-blades he caught one fleeting glimpse of the features of Sexton Blake.

Then the rest of those prone figures came to life, and leaped up. Two of the commissaire's men caught Lacroix, and as Blake released his hold Lacroix felt the touch of cold steel on his wrists. Then he gazed about him in silence. There were Stephen Barclay, with a dead cigar between his lips, Tinker, Graves, and lastly, Count Flambert. It was to him that Lacroix spoke.

"I was afraid in Manila that you were getting out of hand," he said, with an attempt at bravado. "If I had worked more quickly there I should have had you where I wanted you before this meddling Sexton Blake poked his nose in! However, my dear count, you have won out. And the charming Mademoiselle Flambert is lost to me. Alas! But what will you?"

The commissaire tapped him on the shoulder.

"You will have plenty of time later on for that sort of thing, Lacroix," he said curtly. "We don't want to hear it now."

Then he made a sign and as he felt the tug of steel upon his wrists Gaston Lacroix swaggered off between his two guards. He did not even glance at Honan Pierre as he passed him, but he knew how he had been sold out by the half-caste.

He might try to carry it off with a swagger, but already in the mind of Gaston Lacroix was the cold dread of the French penal settlement in New Caledonia—that purgatory of living death to which he knew he must go.

Nor, as he was led down the path to the lane, did he see the crouching figure of Kulai-Tui as she peered out from the concealment of a low hibiscus, her sloe-black eyes half-closed and her throat moving in silent laughter.

•   •   •   •   •

The yacht Fleur-de-Lys remained in Saigon for another two days. It was necessary for Blake to make certain depositions before the Commissaire of Police, and there was some delay over the preliminary examination of Lacroix. But at last officialdom released them, and on a warm, sunny evening the yacht slipped down the Saigon River, bound for Hong Kong.

On the after-deck sat Blake, Yvonne, Graves, the Flamberts, and Stephen Barclay. They had been discussing the last details of the case, but at last Blake dismissed it as he glanced apologetically at Yvonne.

"It was my fault, I am afraid," he said. "I vowed I should not touch any business whatsoever on our holidays, and you see what I led you to, Yvonne."

Yvonne smiled back at him.

"I knew in Manila that you would succumb." she said. Then her eyes grew tender. "And I am glad you did, for you have brought to our friends peace and security at last." And as she spoke she laid one hand on Honore's.

"And more than that," said Count Flambert, rising and standing before Blake. "You have given me the right to lift up my head and gaze fearlessly once more upon the world. Monsieur, I salute you!"

And with that the old man turned and walked to the rail, his emotions too deep for further words.

Blake and Yvonne rose, too, and strolled up the deck together. They paused just beneath the bridge, and as Blake took Yvonne's arm to steady her against the freshening breeze, he lifted his hand and pointed towards the bow.

Ensconced there, apparently oblivious of their surroundings, were Tinker and Betty Barclay, their heads close together and their eyes fixed upon the deepening violet of the Eastern sky.

The sinking sun made a soft halo of the girl's golden head, a halo which seemed to touch the ruffled, darker locks of Sexton Blake's fortunate assistant.

"I'll wager Tinker is not discussing cases now!" remarked Blake, with a smile.

Yvonne's eyes softened. "No, not cases," she said, in a low tone.

They lingered for a moment longer, then, close together, they passed along the deck in silence.

THE END.

[25000 WORDS]

GEORGE MARSDEN PLUMMER and DR. HUXTON RYMER,

The two most cunning and persistent crooks ever encountered by the famous private detective appear in Nos. 228 and 229 of THE SEXTON BLARE LIBRARY. *[229 is The Spirit Smugglers, by Teed /drf.]*

Now on Sale at all Newsagents,

A CHINESE POLICEMAN
(of Shanghai).

Our Magnificent Serial Story of Peril and Adventure in the Mysterious East. This yarn is written by the author of the Yvonne series—it's worth following consistently!

Our Magnificent Serial Story of peril and Adventure in the Mysterious East. This yarn is written by the author of the Yvonne series—it's worth following consistently. *[Hodder says this is <u>written by Teed</u>. Now I find mention of the serial in issues 956 and 977, as perhaps, first and last. 21 issues? /drf]*

WHAT HAS ALREADY HAPPENED.

Jim Moberly, a clerk in a City office, attracts the favourable attention of Lawrence Malone, an explorer of world-wide fame, who is about to start on an important secret political mission into the heart of China. In this mission he is aided by a Chinese secret society known as the Four Lakes Tong, while a rival tong, the Black Valley, seeks to frustrate his plans. After many adventures with One Eye and other enemy members of the Black Talley Tong, Malone and Moberly reach San Francisco. They are each given a secret symbol which will be their passport into the unknown regions of China. Travelling to Honolulu, the enemy's agents capture Malone by a trick and take him to an outlying island. Jim goes in pursuit, and eventually finds his chief locked in a chest, from which he frees him by blowing the lock to pieces. They make their way back to the boat, the Sally, again, and as they come to the beach a strange sight meets their gaze.

(Now read on.)

A Telegram

On the sand lay three prone figures, while a little distance away another Chinaman was dragging himself towards the trees. A little farther on, near the long boat, they could see John and his companions squatting on their heels and apparently cleaning the blades of their knives in the sand. They were going about the business in a cold blooded, matter of fact manner, that sent a queer shiver down Jim's spine.

"Look at that old yellow rascal!" grunted the commodore. "In half an hour he'll be skinning the rest of them at fan-tan as if nothing like a scrap ever took place. He's as deep as the Pacific, is that old Chink!"

"And it is his depth of cunning that saved the Chief," thought Jim, as he looked at the haggard features of the explorer.

On reaching the squatting Celestials, the commodore demanded particulars of the fight. John looked up and waved his hand vaguely in the direction of the trees.

"One, two, tlee, allee samee gone," he said casually. "Allee lest Chineeman makee go look see long tlees."

And that was all the description he ever gave of the fight and the subsequent flight of the Black Valley men. Three of the Sally's crew were wounded, one rather seriously but the Celestials took far less account of that than did the Europeans. When Malone had been assisted into the boat, the wounded were dumped over the gunwale by their fellows, and a moment later they were pulling back towards the Sally.

Up in the bow, John sat polishing the blade of his knife on an old piece of oily rag. Once and once only his oblique eyes rested on Lawrence Malone, but what thoughts were behind that impassive countenance no man could guess.

They made an easy run of it back through the lovely afternoon, but it was well after dark by the time they had slipped past the headland into Honolulu. Malone had had a good sleep on the way, and awoke much refreshed. Following that he and the commodore had a long private talk, but how much of the truth Malone told the other Jim never knew.

The magnate drove them to the dock in his car, and, as they got out, neither Malone nor Jim said much in the way of thanks. It was not necessary with men who understood each other as well as Malone and Morgan. And in his heart of hearts Jim felt sure the magnate had thoroughly enjoyed the expedition. In him was something of the buccaneering spirit of old—a thing in which Jim had a kindred feeling.

As they made their way along the promenade-deck towards the companion way, Jim caught a fleeting glimpse of a Chinaman sitting on the forward-hatch, shaking dice with two other Celestials. It was John.

But no sooner did Malone and Jim reach their cabin than they found, stuck in the side of the washstand, a telegram. Malone tore it open and read the contents hurriedly. Then he turned to Jim.

"Things are getting bad in Hong Kong, Jim. I think we shall have to leave the Ecuador at Yokohama, and get a boat that will run us down direct. It's hard to tell whether One Eye will transfer from the Jap boat to this steamer or not, but we must find out before we sail to-morrow morning."

At Hong-Kong.

LAURENCE MALONE and Jim Moberly were not mistaken in thinking that One Eye would attempt to transfer from the Jap steamer at Honolulu to the Ecuador, for very shortly after they had come aboard a message reached Malone, saying that One Eye had secured a cabin. Jim wasn't sure from whom the warning had come, but he had a shrewd idea that John, the fan-tan player, was responsible for it.

Malone acted promptly.

A short interview with the chief officer, and afterwards with Captain Nelson, proved sufficient, and half an hour later One Eye and his companion were bundled over the side. Malone knew that they would find considerable difficulty in regaining the Jap steamer owing to the hostility of the Four Lakes men in Honolulu, and he hoped that they would be left behind. He was not to know for some weeks whether this had happened or not.

They made the run to Yokohama in exactly thirteen days, with no incident during that time which emanated from the Black Valley Tong. Either the tong men had received orders to defer action until some time later, or else the Four Lakes men on board under the fan-tan player were holding them in check.

They found on arriving at Yokohama, that they could catch a steamer the following day which would take them direct to Hong Kong.

Malone decided to take advantage of this, as to continue by the Ecuador would mean going on from Yokohama to Kobe, thence through the Inland Sea and across the Yellow Sea to Shanghai, from Shanghai down past Formosa to Manila, and, after several days in Manila, back to Hong Kong, which was the last port of call on the outward voyage of the Ecuador. But by changing they could save nearly three weeks, and time was a very important factor just then.

Advices which reached Malone in Yokohama caused the explorer considerable perturbation, and he confided to Jim that things had already begun to move seriously in Canton. The steamer to which they transferred was smaller than the Ecuador, but very comfortable, and as they steamed south Jim began to enjoy things more, as it had been raw and chill at Yokohama.

It was just after noon when the pilot took them into the long, twisting roadstead Hong Kong and jockeyed the ship into action at one of the docks in Kowloon.

It was beautifully cool, for Hong Kong was in the midst of her "winter," and as they crossed from Kowloon in the ferry Jim stood up in the front admiring the towering grandeur of the peak which dominates the whole island. Along the waterfront were all the commercial houses of the Europeans while off to the left was the thickly-scattered native quarter, which was also repeated on the right.

Straight up the side of the mountain Jim could see the ever-narrowing rails of the Pent railway, and scattered along the whole slope were the bungalows of the European element —the Portuguese, and even the wealthy Chinese and Japanese, Malone explained how they were laid out, with the Europeans keeping strictly to their own level of the mountain.

They landed at the little jetty in front of the Phœnix Club, and when their luggage had been handed over to the coolies, they entered rickshaws and drove along the front to the Hong Kong Hotel. They secured rooms there, and after a rapid change, descended to the lounge, where Malone ordered tea.

Malone had selected a table in a quiet corner of the lounge from where it was easy for them to see everyone who passed through, but which, on the other hand, was out of the line of vision of the main passage.

The Chinese "boy" took their order, and a few minutes later brought the tray. He set it down and departed, while Malone prepared to pour out the tea. As he did so, however, he found underneath the tea pot a small folded piece of paper. He palmed it quickly with his left hand, and did not look at it until he had filled both cups.

On a table near by were some old London illustrated journals, and reaching out, Malone picked up one of these. Using it as a shield, he unfolded the note. It proved to be a fantastic-looking scrawl in Chinese characters.

Malone tore the paper into tiny shreds which he thrust into his pocket. Jim looked at him inquiringly.

"We leave just before dawn to-morrow morning, Jim," said Malone, in a low tone. "I will tell you about it later. But we shall have to leave the hotel at three o'clock in the morning."

They finished their tea, and afterwards walked along to the Hong Kong Club, of which Malone was a member. They remained there until nearly dinner-time, for Malone ran into several old friends. The one topic of conversation was of the condition of things in the interior of China, and, although Malone listened closely to everything that was said, and offered no argument to the various theories advanced, he said not the slightest word that would indicate that he and Jim were bound for the interior.

They were pressed to remain and dine, but Malone shook his head. They had arrived too late in the day to find the Hong Kong office of Wallace, Marshall & Co., open, and while he was changing, Malone had sent off an urgent message to Kirby, the manager in Hong Kong. He expected an answer by the time he got back to the hotel, for it was essential that he should get possession of the registered packet which Jim had posted in London before they left for Canton.

On reaching the hotel they found Kirby himself sitting in the lounge awaiting their return. He greeted Malone warmly, and when the latter had explained that not only was Jim his assistant, but that he had also been employed in the London office of the firm, Kirby gave the young man a hearty welcome. They talked of the men in the London office, and "shop" generally, for some little time, until Malone finally broached the reason for his note being of such an urgent nature.

Kirby nodded his head at once. "There are some letters, and I think one or two cablegrams for you at the office," he said. "I think there is also a cable for you, Moberly. I shall take a rickshaw at once and bring everything back to you."

"What about money?" asked Malone. "I have a draft on you, but I don't want it all at present. What I should like is an order on your Canton correspondents for some silver coin. I shall need a considerable quantity."

"I can arrange that for you. When are you leaving?"

"At daybreak. This is strictly confidential, Kirby. We are going up by junk, and I don't want it known."

"That's all right. I will bring you back an order on our Canton people to pay you as much silver coin as you require, and I will also advise them by telegram early in the morning in case they haven't enough actual coin in hand."

"Thank you!" Malone and Jim did not change for dinner, and, instead of dining in the main dining-room on the first floor they went into the buffet which was off the passage just beyond the bar. They had finished, and were back in the lounge smoking when Kirby returned.

Jim waited while Malone and Kirby went up to the former's room to complete their business. From where he was sitting he could look out into the street that ran past the main entrance of the hotel. The lobby was brightly lighted and outside the door a large arc-lamp was hanging.

Jim was idly watching the flow of mixed Oriental humanity past the door, when suddenly he saw a dark, sinister countenance turned full upon him. For a moment only it was there, then it disappeared and was lost in the crowd.

But Jim Moberly knew that in that brief pause One Eye had looked straight at him and had recognised him.

In the Junk to Wuchow.

JIM did not communicate his discovery to Malone until Kirby had taken his departure. When he did so the explorer did not seem much surprised.

"I half expected that," he remarked. "That means he was able to regain the Jap steamer in Honolulu. I didn't notice it either lying at one of the buoys in the harbour or in dock at Kowloon, but it may have arrived here some days ago and departed. But as far as Hong Kong is concerned we shall have to trust to our own guards. The whole native district is seething with intrigue and plotting, and we must slip through before trouble breaks out in the form of a general riot. If we don't we may be stranded here for weeks. Now come along up to my room, Jim. We have a good deal of work to do yet."

On the table in Malone's room was a large map of Southern China. From the envelope which Jim had posted in London Malone took the precious paper bearing the exact latitude and longitude of the spot which was their objective. Then, at Malone's request, Jim handed over the tiny chamois bag which he had received from Wong Tu in San Francisco.

As Malone opened the bag and drew out a folded piece of waxed paper, Jim bent forward eagerly, for it was the first time he had seen that which he had guarded so carefully.

Malone opened it up, and Jim saw that it was a tiny plan of some sort. It consisted of a series of crosses and lists, while in one corner were some Chinese characters

Malone studied it closely for some time, then he turned to Jim.

"Come closer, Jim," he said; "what I have to tell you must be said in a whisper. The information I am going to give you is the final revelation of why we are here, and why we are going into the interior of China. If I go under, then you must try your best to carry through the work."

"I understand that, Chief." answered Jim quietly. "I will try to finish things as you would have them finished."

"I rely on you. Now listen!"

For several minutes Malone talked to Jim in whispers, but so slowly did he enunciate that every syllable reached Jim clearly. When Malone had finished, he said:

"Do you understand?"

"Perfectly, Chief."

"And it is quite clear how you are to act in case anything happens to me!"

"Quite clear."

"Then remember each of the details I have given you. From now on we must both carry them only in our mind."

With that the explorer took out a box of matches. He made a small pile of torn paper in a saucer as he destroyed the two precious bits of information, then he set it afire, and not until the last tiny bit was reduced to ashes did he remove his eyes from the saucer. Finally, he rubbed the ashes to dust between his fingers, and taking the saucer to the window, threw the contents out into the night.

At half-past two in the morning Malone woke Jim, instructing him to dress in khaki breeches and shirt, and leather leggings. They had bought a couple of Stetson hats in Chicago, which were also to form part of their equipment, while each carried his automatic, fully loaded, slung under his left arm, where it was inconspicuous. The rest of their luggage they locked, and left in their rooms, although Jim found later that it was to follow them in some mysterious fashion, for the next time he saw it was after they had passed through some very strenuous experiences. They passed quietly through the silent lobby, where a single light burned. They emerged by a side door, and, after walking a short distance, turned a corner.

There they found two rickshaws waiting, each with three coolies in attendance. Malone entered one, and Jim climbed into the other. No words were spoken, but as soon as they were in, the rickshaws started.

It was dark and chill, but out in the harbour Jim could see the lights of the ships riding at the mooring-buoys there, while on the other side were the water-front lights of Kowloon.

He had not questioned Malone as to their exact destination, but soon he saw that the rickshaw coolies were trotting at a steady pace towards the eastern end of the town.

They passed several big Chinese restaurants where the lights were still ablaze, then they swung upwards towards a dark road that skirted the edge of the mountain. A little later and they had left the town behind. Then it was a steady journey between overhanging trees, until eventually Jim found they were descending. Suddenly, he realised where they were bound.

As they steamed in, past the point of the island, Malone had pointed out different places of interest to Jim, among which had been the distant point, behind which lay the little Chinese fishing village of Aberdeen. And now, as they descended towards the shore, Jim saw against the starlit sky a perfect forest of junk-masts. He opined that the junk which they were to board was one of those.

And he was right. As they reached the shore the rickshaws came to a stop. Malone and Jim got out, and the next second the two vehicles had started off through the night. One Chinese stood holding the short painter, while a second stood in the stern with an oar ready. They climbed in, and the first Celestial pushed off.

They were sculled quietly between the confusing multitude of junks until they were near the outer fringe of the anchored craft. Then they drew in beside one which had been dragged round ready to slip out on the first ebb of the tide.

As they climbed up a rope ladder and went over the side, Jim felt first stirrings of a light breeze which was coming down from the mountain. He saw several celestials moving about the deck, but they paid not the slightest attention to either of the Europeans.

Malone led the way towards the high pooped stern, where a Chinaman suddenly emerged from the shadows. He lifted a bamboo-and-grass mat which hung over the entrance to what he called the cabin of the junk, and with a warning word to Jim, the explorer felt for the rungs of the ladder which led below. Jim followed his leader, and presently found himself in a low cabin, which was provided with two mat beds, a rough teak table, and, strangely enough, their own "hold alls," which held each a pillow and blanket.

The place was lit by a single oil lantern which hung from the ceiling, and was filled with the heavy odour of burning joss-sticks, and something else, which Jim now recognised as opium.

"Might as well turn in, Jim," remarked Malone, as he began to open his hold-all. "We can't show ourselves on deck until we are well clear of Hong Kong, so we might as well try and get some sleep."

Jim followed the suggestion, and five minutes later each was stretched out on one of the mat beds. The sound of creaking blocks and cordage came faintly from the deck, and a slight movement of the junk told Jim that they were getting under way.

Then he drifted off into a sound sleep, in which he struggled with innumerable Chinese hordes, until he woke to find Malone shaking him by the shoulder.

"Well, you have slept!" exclaimed the explorer, as Jim sat up. "It is afternoon. If you want to see Macao and the entrance to the river, come up on deck. We will have some food presently."

Jim rolled off the bed, and followed Malone up the ladder.

On reaching the deck he found that they were scudding along under a steady southeast breeze that was flicking the China Sea about them in flying spray, and causing the old mat sails of the crazy-looking junk to stretch and strain alarmingly. But the junk was making progress at a rate that astonished Jim. Forward the crew was gathered, while aft a Celestial bent over the long tiller in the peculiar fashion in which all the Chinese steer.

Malone pointed over the port quarter.

"There is Macao," he said. "It is, as you perhaps know, a Portuguese possession and rather a quaint place. On our return—if we do return—I shall try and take you there. Its gambling is its chief industry now, but there are some very interesting old Portuguese remains. There, ahead of you, is the entrance to the river. It doesn't appear so from here; but it is. You will be able to see it better in another hour or so. If this wind holds we will get well up the river by evening, and, with the sweeps out, will make Canton during the night."

Jim leant over the rail, watching the unfolding panorama of the flat river banks, until he saw a Celestial coming along the deck with two big soup-plates full of steaming food. He found that he was ravenous, and needed no urging to follow Malone below.

It was Jim's first introduction to real Chinese food, and he looked at it suspiciously until Malone assured him that it contained neither dead rats nor hundred-year-old eggs.

Jim sampled it tentatively, and, to his astonishment, found it delicious. He discovered that it was simply turtle-and-chicken stew done with vegetables, rice, and peppers, over which thick brown gravy had been poured.

Malone smiled when he saw that Jim left not a single scrap.

They returned to the deck, where they idled and smoked until a low-voiced warning from the steersman caused Malone to look forward.

"Down below, Jim!" he ordered curtly, "Here comes the evening steamer from Canton to Hong Kong!"

They dodged below, and remained there until dusk had fallen. The breeze still held, and, true to Malone's prophecy, they made Canton that night.

They dared not risk going ashore; but Malone had two visits during the evening, both of his visitors being Chinese. Long and earnest conversations took place in the cabin, and Jim gathered that, so far, things were moving smoothly. They lay out in the river mist all night, but at the first break of dawn got under way again.

Down in the cabin Malone explained what the next move on the journey was to be.

"We shall have to work the river in the junk as far as Wuchow," he said. "It will take us from ten days to two weeks to do it, even if we have favourable weather. But the junk will be much safer that risking a power-boat.

"At Wuchow we shall leave the junk, as that is the end of the junk navigation. We shall pick up some of our luggage there, and then continue up the river in a small boat as far as Kweilin. That is about two hundred miles from Wuchow, and there we will be in the midst of the most dangerous part of the river passage.

"The river is full of shoals and rapids, and is infested by river pirates. They, together with Black Valley men, acting as pirates, will be our chief danger, but I have formed a plan which I hope will be the means of outwitting them. If we can get through that two hundred miles safely, then it will be a race from Kweilin to our destination. No matter what happens, I want you to take things as they come, and show no surprise at anything.

Malone's estimate was not far wrong, for it took them sixteen days to work up the river to Wuchow. It was a dreary, monotonous passage after the novelty wore off, although Jim copied Malone's philosophic attitude, and showed no signs of chafing. The only amusement was watching the other junks and sampans on the river and the queer-looking, straggling towns and villages on the banks of the river.

At nights they would often tie up in the midst of other junks and sampans, and, lying down in the cabin, Jim would listen to the low, constant murmur of the invisible life about him. It was weird and sinister, and as they got deeper and deeper into the heart of the Yellow Empire he realised acutely how completely cut off from their own kind he and Malone were getting.

He was in the midst of a water-life, where whole families were born, lived, and died aboard the river craft, with scarcely ever setting foot on the shore. It was a distinctly peculiar element of life in the country of the dragon, where a year's pay might amount to no more than a dollar, and where each and every one of those beings would cheerfully slit a dozen throats for half that sum.

As they got higher and higher up the Kwang-Si, Malone insisted that they should remain more and more in the concealment of the cabin, and only at night did they have any real freedom of movement.

Then, at last, the seemingly interminable journey came to an end, and one evening at sunset they tied up in the outer fringe of the vast medley of river craft which lay at Wuchow.

Jim noticed now that Malone moved with an ever greater caution. Not until it was quite dark would he permit Jim to go on deck, and even then he made him don a wide grass hat, such as the junk crew wore. From the junk, Jim could see the distant lights of the town, but an early night mist soon cut it off from his view. Malone was pacing up and down the deck impatiently, and from what he had said Jim knew that he was expecting advices of some sort during the evening.

It was just after nine o'clock when a sampan slipped out of the mist and struck softly against the side of the junk. Over the side came a shadowy figure. It joined with that of Malone, and the two descended to the cabin.

It was about a quarter of an hour later when Malone reappeared. The visitor disappeared over the side, and Malone came along to where Jim was standing.

"It is both good news and bad, Jim," he said, in a low tone. "The plans I have made are ready for execution, and I hope will go through all right. But One Eye arrived in Wuchow two days ago. We seem to have given him the slip on our way up the river, and he travelled on by sampan. He has left Wuchow, and is on his way up the river to Kweilin.

"If the road from Wuchow to Kweilin was possible, I would change our plans and go that way. But I am advised that it is impassable, and that it is infested with thousands of disbanded soldiers, so we shall have to stick to the river. Now let us turn in, for we get away by sampan early in the morning."

They went below, where they smoked a final pipe before laying out their blankets. Jim, who was by now thoroughly at home in the junk, dropped off to sleep very soon, but not so Malone. He lay on his mat bed for some time, gazing up at the rough beams above him. When Jim's regular breathing told him the lad slept, he got softly to the floor, and stole across the cabin.

On a small wooden stool lay Jim's coat, and under that was his belt and holster, with the automatic in it. Working very quietly, Malone drew the pistol from the holster, and took out the loaded clip. Removing the cartridges one by one, he dropped them into his pocket. Then he worked the slide until he had thrown out the cartridge in the breach. That done, he took several blank shells from his pocket and refilled the clip, throwing one into the breech as before. Then he replaced the automatic in the holster, and stole back to his bed. Seating himself there, he went through exactly the same process with his own weapon. When he had finished, he smiled grimly and lay down.

"Now for it!" he muttered. "If there is a hitch, Jim and I will be up against it hard with nothing but blanks to shoot, but we must take the risk."

Then he closed his eyes, and dozed.

•   •   •   •   •

Jim Moberly was in the midst of a fantastic dream which turned to startling reality as he came up on his bed at the sound of a medley of shrill squeals and shouts. Malone was also sitting up, and each reached for his automatic at the same moment.

On deck pandemonium seemed to have broken loose. Crash followed crash, and the shouts and screams increased in volume every moment. Half the river people seemed to have made an assault on the junk, and even as Jim and Malone came to their feet, a horde of wild-looking Celestials came crashing through the opening from the deck without waiting to use the ladder.

Malone had jumped for the centre of the cabin, and Jim joined him. Together they raised their weapons, and began to fire. Straight at the oncoming mob Jim aimed, and time after time he pulled the trigger. But, though his pistol cracked in a rapid sequence of explosions, he did not seem to be doing much damage.

Nor did Malone seem to be faring any better, for as he fired his last cartridge and turned his pistol to club it, the crowd reached them, and the next moment Jim was fighting desperately with half a dozen squealing Chinks forcing him back on to the mat bed. He fought gamely, and sent his fist crashing again and again into the press of yellow faces which seemed to be jerking about all around him.

He had one glimpse of Malone hurling the Celestials right and left, then a crushing wave of yellow humanity descended upon Jim, and he went down. The next moment something was pressed over his mouth and he went sailing a way through a sea of yellow mist.

THE PRISON ON THE MOORS

This is the third of Mr. T. C. Bridges interesting articles on Dartmoor, the largest and oldest of our British Penal Establishments. In his previous talks he has traced the history of the place from the time it was built to house the French prisoners of war after the battles with Napoleon, and described the hard lot of the convicts imprisoned there under the old system of punishment. In this article he shows something of the conditions prevailing to-day.

THE STONE-YARD.

This exclusive U. J. photo shows the dreaded " Stone-Yard " referred to in this article. Notice the hammers chained to each block of stone, so that they may not be used as weapons of offence against the watching warders.

The Stone-Yard—Dartmoor in War-time—Juvenile Adults—A Prisoner's Ruse—Improved Conditions—Reformation not Revenge

IN last week's article I dealt with "ticket of leave." I explained this fully, because I wanted to state that the punishments awarded of late years for breaches of prison discipline are no longer long confinement in a punishment cell, but loss of marks implying a loss of stage and remission.

If the offence is a serious one, such as an assault on a warder, the prisoner gets "cells" into the bargain, and when in a punishment cell his diet is very plain fare.

But while in old days the governor of a prison could order a flogging, nowadays he can do nothing of the sort.

He has to bring the offender before a board of visiting justices, and even if they sentence a man to be flogged, the order has first to be confirmed by the Home Secretary. Fifty years ago men were flogged every day. Now in all the prisons in the kingdom I don't suppose there are six floggings in the year.

At Dartmoor, if a man tries to escape he is not flogged. He gets cells for perhaps forty days, and he may be sentenced to wear leg irons for six months, and a punishment dress. A man who has assaulted a warder or another prisoner will probably get a similar punishment.

Among black sheep there are always blacker.

Inside Dartmoor Prison is a small yard where ordinary visitors are never taken. In it a dozen or so sullen-faced men sit, each in a separate niche, cracking stone. The hammers are each chained to blocks of stone, and warders watch the stone-breakers all day.

These are the incorrigibles—men of such brutal temper that they dare not be trusted to work with their fellows.

Every one of them has been guilty of savage assaults. They are human wild beasts, and must be treated as such.

During the war, Dartmoor was turned into a place of confinement for Conscientious Objectors.

Of these, perhaps the less said the better, but in order to show local feeling on the subject, I will merely mention the fact that, when the first batch of "old lags" returned, the village children gathered and cheered them!

During the war our prison population diminished by more than fifty per cent, which just shows that, when there is work for everyone, people have no time for crime.

IN THE QUARRIES.

A very large amount of stone is quarried annually at Dartmoor. This sketch, drawn from a photograph, gives a good general idea of the place.

THE STONE-YARD.

This exclusive U. J. photo shows the dreaded "Stone-Yard" referred to in this article. Notice the hammers chained to each block of stone, so that they may not be used as weapons of offence against the watching warders.

The J.A.'s.

Now, alas! the numbers are mounting up again, but the increase is not as great as it might seem on the surface, for Portland, which for years has been the great "star" prison, has now been turned into a Borstal institute, and a number of its former inhabitants have been drafted to Dartmoor.

Nowadays the convict population of Dartmoor is about seven hundred. It consists, as before, mainly of "recidivists," old lags, but there are also a small number of "Juvenile Adults," commonly called J. A.'s.

There are boys of seventeen to twenty-one, who have committed offences sufficiently serious to merit sentences of penal servitude. Quite a number are murderers. These are usually crimes of jealousy. They have either killed their sweethearts or else their rivals. Many are sentenced for life.

These young prisoners are kept under a modified Borstal system. They have different workshops from the old lags, and separate instructors.

They have a gymnasium of their own, and in the evenings those who have earned the privilege by good conduct are allowed to sit in a sort of common-room, where they may play draughts and other games under the eyes of their schoolmaster.

All have regular schooling, and each is instructed in a trade. These boys have the care of the prison horses, and, as a rule, look after them very well. They do all the shoeing. They have a very fine carpenter's shop, where they are taught cabinet-making, wood carving, and the like.

Some very fine specimens of their work are to be seen in the prison chapel.

To a visitor the "shops" are the most interesting part of a convict prison like Dartmoor.

In a "local" prison, such as Wandsworth, the terms of imprisonment are too short to give time to teach the inmates trades. But since the shortest sentence of penal servitude is three years, in a convict prison a lot more can be done in that respect, and in some of the shops you can see skill of a high order, which, in many cases, is the means of erstwhile criminals gaining an honest living after release by following the trade they learned in prison.

At Dartmoor the principal indoor trades are tailoring, tin-smithery, and the making of Post Office bags and string. There is also a boot-making shop, and one for bookbinding, besides the blacksmiths' forges and the places where carpentry and basket-making are taught.

Taking No Risks.

At Dartmoor tin utensils are made not only for Dartmoor Prison, but for others as well. All the food is served in tin plates and mugs, while the knives also are of tin.

It may easily be understood that it does not do to allow convicts earthenware or china, which might be broken up to serve as dangerous weapons.

As for steel, any man is promptly punished who is found in possession of any sharp instrument. Yet, even so, many risk trouble simply for the sake of vanity. A man will get a piece of hoop-iron and grind it down to razor-like sharpness just so as to get a shave instead of the usual beard-cutting with scissors, which is the rule in all convict prisons.

I might mention that in pre-war days every man was carefully searched ("rubbed down," as it was called), twice a day by a warder, so as to make sure that he had no contraband about him.

That searching has now been abolished, but all cells are constantly searched during the absence of their inmates. Certain warders are detailed for this purpose, and become amazingly expert.

Yet, to show the difficulty of dealing with convicts, I can tell you of a man who utterly defeated the searchers. A bar in his cell window was found cut nearly through, and he was had up before the governor, who asked him where he kept his file.

He refused to say, and was punished and changed to another cell.

Again a bar was ground out, and again he was punished and sent to a cell where there was no possibility of escape. When his term was up and he was having his final interview with the governor, the latter said to him:

"Out of curiosity, Jones. I should be interested to know where you kept that file."

The man smiled, and, putting his hand into his mouth, drew out a small watchmaker's file. Incredible as it may appear, he had kept that file tied to a back tooth and hanging down inside his throat.

The shops are large and airy, and compare favourably with those in the ordinary factory.

In all prisons silence is the rule, yet it is a rule more often broken than observed. Of course, in the shop, where there is constant hammering, the men talk almost as they like.

Lip-Language.

In the tailors' shop it is different. You go in, look round, see rows of men sitting cross-legged on the board, stitching away, and are conscious of a curious, low hum. Yet not a single pair of lips is moving.

The fact is that these men have all learned to talk without moving their lips. They are probably discussing you, and perhaps saying very uncomplimentary things about you, yet you cannot hear one single word.

All the warders' uniforms are made in the tailors' shops. So are the convicts' clothes. Even the washing is done in the prison.

A big prison like Dartmoor is a little self-contained world which makes its own clothes and boots, feeds and kills its own pigs, shoes its own horses and builds the farm-carts, makes its own gas, even builds all necessary new buildings and repairs the old ones.

You can find inside the prison men of every trade. Whether you want a notice printed or a telephone repaired, a man can always be found to do it.

In the old days a well managed prison paid for itself. Wakefield Gael, where an enterprising governor started a furniture factory, used even to return a handsome profit. Then the Trade Unions decided that no prison goods should be sold in the open market, so that nowadays prison work is all done for Government, and, as a result, each prisoner costs the taxpayer a heavy sum annually.

The actual value of a prisoner's labour does not cover half the cost of his keep, plus the expenses of housing and looking after him.

I was speaking of the improved conditions which convicts enjoy since the war. One of these is the shortening of the hours of work. A prisoner gets up early, usually at half-past five. He has his breakfast, cleans his cell, and then goes to chapel.

It is not until nearly nine that he gets to his day's work. Then he has only three hours, for, in order to arrange for the warders to get their dinners in two shifts, the parties do not go out again until two o'clock.

The outdoor parties knock off in winter at four o'clock, because the authorities do not wish to risk them being caught by darkness before reaching the prison.

Before five the men are all back in their cells; then supper is served, and at eight lights are extinguished and silence reigns.

More Humane Warders.

The second, and perhaps most important change, is in the matter of food.

Bacon is given in the morning and cheese for supper. The midday meal now includes not only green vegetables, but on several days of the week pudding. On Fridays fresh fish is served. The food is all of good quality, and many people are inclined to think that it is too good.

But there are two sides to that question.

Imprisonment means that a man is turned into a machine. He lives under constant restraint and has to obey every order given him. He cannot even write a letter or receive one without that letter going under the eyes of the governor or deputy. Conditions are hard enough without them being aggravated by bad or insufficient food.

A third and very great improvement is the changed relations between warders and prisoners.

At Dartmoor in particular the type of warder to-day is a very much better one than it was twenty-five years ago. There are men doing ordinary warder work who were commissioned officers during the Great War. Such men naturally endeavour to lead rather than drive, and although a warder is forbidden to talk with a convict, except to give him instructions or orders, this is another rule the breach of which is winked at to some extent. A prisoner who behaves himself gets many a kindly word from the officer in charge of his party, and the result is a better feeling all through the prison.

Any prisoner who wishes can put his name down to see the governor or the doctor, and if he has any real complaint, he is sure of a sympathetic hearing.

For instance, a man hears that one of his family is ill, and asks that he may receive special news. Such a request, if genuine, is sure to be granted.

If a man goes sick, the doctor sees him. Should the complaint be serious he is sent straight to hospital, a hospital which compares with any in the land, and where, if his condition demands it, he will be fed on chicken and port wine. If it is merely a cold, he will stay in bed in his cell for a day or two.

As for the chaplains, they are constantly visiting from cell to cell, and always ready to talk to a man who wants a chat. It is very seldom that they meet with rudeness. They manage the library, and a man can have any books he likes within reason.

Sounds All Right, But—

Yet, in spite of all these indulgences, please do not run away with the idea that life as a convict in a convict prison is a picnic.

For an educated man, the mere fact that he is obliged to associate with the scum of the earth is a hideous punishment. For all the discipline is hard. A prisoner can hardly call his soul his own. Every single thing he does from getting up in the morning to lying down at night is by an order.

If you happen to be at Princetown railway station when an old lag who has been released is starting off for London or wherever he is going, you will notice that he is like a lost child.

He has forgotten how to do the ordinary things of life. He could hardly buy his own ticket. He stands, waiting for orders, lost, because there is no longer anyone to give them.

Men like this have precious little chance of making an honest livelihood, especially since they are on licence, and bound to report to the police at regular intervals. Nearly always they drop again into crime, and are rapidly back in prison.

It would really be more kind to keep these old offenders in custody for good. There is a move to do this, under what is called "The Indeterminate Sentence."

But of this and of Camp Hill Prison, where these old offenders are sent, I shall have something more to say.

Next Thursday's Article: PARKHURST, the ISLAND PRISON. By T. C. Bridges.

No. 3.   Presented with the UNION JACK Library for the week ending May 20th, 1922.

ONE OF THE HALLS AT DARTMOOR.

Along both sides of each gallery the convicts' cells are ranged. Note the wire netting below, so placed that inmates may not commit suicide by jumping from the galleries.

The Life-Story of Charles Peace

Compiled and written by the late H. B. Irving, who was a noted criminologist.

Last week's article, which contained the account of Charles Peace's early career, told how he originally entered the ranks of crime in his native town of Sheffield and how he was led to commit his first murder at Manchester, for which two brothers of the name of Habron were arrested and put on trial. The following account describes how he himself attended the trial, and, later, his descent upon London.

A Miscarriage of Justice—The Lure of the Dysons—Wanderings—Life in London—A Double Life—The Unsuspected "Mr. Thompson."

FOLLOWING the arrest of the brothers John and William Habron for the murder of the policeman he had shot in Manchester, Charles Peace looked forward eagerly to the forthcoming trial, which was to open at Manchester on November 27th.

Peace attended the trial, there to hear John Habron acquitted and William Habron sentenced to death. The latter's sentence was subsequently commuted to penal servitude for life, and, later still, after Peace's final capture, he was released and given £800 compensation.

On November 29th Peace was in Sheffield. He spent the day in a public-house at Eccleshall, entertaining the customers by playing tunes on a suspended poker, being rewarded with drinks. It took little drink to excite Peace.

At a quarter to seven Peace went to a friend's house, but he was not at home; and, at a loose end, he found the lure of the Dysons irresistible, and at a little before eight o'clock he was watching the house from a passage-way at the back.

He saw Mrs. Dyson come out of the back door and go to an outhouse. He waited, and when she came out, confronted her, holding his revolver in his hand.

"Speak," he said, "or I'll fire!" Mrs. Dyson went back into the outhouse, and Dyson, having heard the disturbance, came into the yard.

Peace made for the passage, and Dyson followed. Peace fired once, the shot striking the passage doorway; but Dyson, undaunted, still followed.

Then Peace, according to his custom, fired a second time, and Dyson fell, shot through the temple, dying two hours afterwards.

The murderer then returned to Sheffield, saw his mother and brother, told them what he had done, and bade them a hasty goodbye.

He walked to Attercliffe Station and booked to Beverley, but left the train at Normanton and went on to York, spending the night in the station yard.

In the morning he took the first train to Beverley, and from there travelled via Collingham to Hull.

Going straight to his wife's eating-house, he demanded dinner, but had hardly commenced to eat it when two detectives came into the shop.

Wooing by Pistol.

He escaped from their exhaustive search by getting on the roof and hiding behind a chimney-stack, and a second time during that day had to repeat the experience.

For some three weeks, however, he contrived to remain in Hull. He shaved his beard, dyed his hair, and for the first time made use of his singular power of contorting his features in such a way as to change altogether the character of his face.

But the hue and cry after him was unremitting. There was a price of £100 on his head, and the walls were placarded with his description.

One means of identification, the loss of a finger, Peace concealed by means of a false arm of gutta percha, ending in a hook, By means of this hook Peace could wield a fork and do other dexterous feats.

Marked man as he was, Peace felt it dangerous to stay longer in Hull than he could help. During the closing days of 1876 and the beginning of 1877 he was continually on the move.

He travelled to Doncaster, and from there to London, where he took train to Bristol. From Bristol he went to Bath, then by way of Didcot to Oxford, and from Birmingham.

Here he stayed only four or five days, then a week in Derby, and on January 9th he arrived in Nottingham, finding convenient lodgings in the house of Mrs. Adamson, a receiver of stolen goods.

It was here that Peace met the woman who was to subsequently betray his identity to the police.

She was at this time about thirty-five years of age, described as "taking" in appearance, of a fair complexion, and rather well educated. She had had a somewhat chequered married life with a man named Bailey, who made her an allowance till she passed under Peace's protection,

Peace declared his passion for her by threatening to shoot her if she did not become his. His apology so melted her heart that she consented to pose as his wife, and from that moment became known to history as Mrs. Thompson.

To London.

Life in Nottingham was varied pleasantly by burglaries carried out with the help of information supplied by Mrs. Adamson. But once Peace was nearly detected, and returned for a short season to Hull, where he lodged in the house of a sergeant of police.

One day Mrs. Peace received a pencilled note saying, "I am waiting to see you just up Anlaby Road." She went there with her son, Willie Ward, and there, to their astonishment, stood her husband, a distinguished figure in black coat and trousers, top hat, velvet waistcoat, with stick, kid gloves, and a pretty little fox terrier by his side.

Peace told them of his whereabouts in the town, but did not disclose to them the fact that his "wife" was there also. To the police-sergeant, his landlord, he described himself as an agent.

The shops still showed the bills offering a reward for his capture, but he plied his usual occupation, and a number of sensational and successful burglaries soon revealed the presence in Hull of no ordinary robber.

Peace had narrow escapes, but with the help of his revolver, and once through the pusillanimity of a policeman, always succeeded in getting away in safety, till he judged it safe for him and Mrs. Thompson to return to Nottingham.

Here, as a result of further exploits, he found an additional reward of £50 offered for his capture. Once detectives surprised him in bed.

He refused to get up and dress in the presence of the detectives, who were obliging enough to go downstairs and wait, and he seized the opportunity to slip out of the house to another part of the town.

From there he sent a note insisting on Mrs. Thompson joining him, and they went to Hull.

But the police, whom he designated a "lot of fools," still frequented his wife's shop, so he determined to quit the north for good and begin life afresh in the ampler and safer field of London.

A Short Career.

Peace's career in London extended over nearly two years, from the beginning of the year 1877 until October, 1878, but they were years of copious achievement. In that time he passed from a poor and obscure lodging in a slum in Lambeth to the state and opulence of a comfortable suburban residence in Peckham.

As a dealer in musical instruments he sallied forth night after night from No. 25, Stangate Street, Lambeth, and raided houses in Camberwell and other parts of South London.

So successful did "business" prove, that at the Christmas of 1877 he invited his daughter and her betrothed to come from Hull and spend the festive season with him. Then for more than one reason he was desirous to unite under the same roof Mrs. Peace and Mrs. Thompson, and, affairs still prospering, he found himself able to move from Lambeth to Crane Court, Greenwich, and before long to take a couple of adjoining houses in Billingsgate Street in the same district, which he furnished in style. He shared one with Mrs. Thompson, while Mrs. Peace and her son Willie were persuaded, after some difficulty, to leave Hull and come to London to dwell in the other.

Pleasant Social Resort.

But Greenwich was not to the taste of Mrs. Thompson, and at her wish Peace removed the whole party to No. 5, East Terrace, Evelina Road, Peckham. Though all living in the same house, Mrs. Peace, who passed as Mrs. Ward, and her son Willie inhabited the basement, while Peace and Mrs. Thompson occupied the best rooms on the ground floor. The house was furnished in the style to confirm "Mr. Thompson's" description of himself as a gentleman of independent means with a taste for scientific inventions.

At the time of his capture Peace was actually engaged on some inventions, among them a smoke helmet for firemen, an improved brush for washing railway-carriages, and a form of hydraulic tank.

Socially he became quite a figure in the neighbourhood. He attended regularly the evening services at the parish church. He was generous in giving and punctual in paying. He had his eccentricities, his love of birds and animals being remarkable. Cats, dogs, rabbits, guinea-pigs, canaries, parrots, and cockatoos, all found hospitality under his roof. It was certainly eccentricity in "Mr. Thompson" that he should wear different coloured wigs and that his dark complexion should suggest the use of walnut juice.

No. 5, East Terrace, Evelina Road, became a pleasant social resort for neighbours, who, however, were always out of the house by half-past ten, as their host's health would not stand late hours. But pleasant as the life was, it was not without its jars, chiefly due to the drunken habits of Mrs. Thompson.

Peace was willing to overlook her failing so long as it was confined to the house, but she had an unfortunate habit of slipping out in an intoxicated condition and chattering to the neighbours.

As she was the repository of many a dangerous secret, the inconvenience of this habit was serious, and Mrs. Thompson on many occasions was followed by Peace or his wife, brought back home, and soundly beaten.

Close Call

Night after night, with few intervals for repose, he would sally forth on a plundering adventure. If the job was a distant one he would take his pony and trap. His range of activities extended as far as Southampton, Portsmouth, and Southsea, but the bulk of his work was done in Blackheath, Streatham, Denmark Hill, and other parts of South London.

All this time the police were busily seeking Charles Peace, the murderer of Mr. Dyson. On one occasion a detective who had known Peace in Yorkshire met him in Farringdon Road, and pursued him up the steps of Holborn Viaduct, but just as the officer, at the top of the steps, reached out and was on the point of grabbing his man, Peace, with lightning-like agility, slipped through his fingers and disappeared. The police never had the slightest suspicion that Mr. Thompson of Peckham was Charles Peace of Sheffield.

However, he made the mistake of outstaying his welcome in South-East London. During the last three months of his career Blackheath was agog at the number of successful burglaries committed in the very midst of its peaceful residents. The vigilance of the local police was aroused, the officers on night duty were only too anxious to effect the capture of the mysterious criminal.

Part 3 of Charles Peace's life-story will appear in next week's Detective Magazine. It will tell of his final exploit, his arrest and execution, and will conclude the series.

20 **The U.J. DETECTIVE MAGAZINE** *Supplement*

FINGER PRINTS

AND ALL ABOUT THEM

In this, the third article in this fascinating series, you are initiated into one or two facts regarding the primary type—one of the four—called Loops. The other types, Arches, Whorls and Composites, will be touched on later. Like the other contents of the U.J. these Finger-Print talks are written to appeal to readers of all ages. They are not only interesting, but are written clearly so as to be easily understood. They provide an easy road to a knowledge of this absorbing subject, the like of which is seldom or never attempted.

Loops the most common Type—The "Fixed Points"—Inner and Outer Termini— "Ulnar" and "Radial" —Simpler than it seems.

To the unskilled observer one fingerprint, with its maze of confusing lines and its complexity of patterning looks very much like another. They are instantly distinguishable, however, to the man who knows where to look, and what to look for, amidst the apparently meaningless mass of lines.

If this were not so finger-prints would be valueless in the work of crime-detection. The mere fact that no one print is exactly the same as one from another finger would be useless, for the main purpose to which police collections are put is to discover quickly whether or not the finger-prints of a prisoner are already on the files, so as to establish his real identity in spite of aliases.

This rapid turning-up of a given set of prints is of course attained by classification and sub-classification.

Now it has been shown in a previous article that all finger-prints are divided into four primary types—Loop, Arch, Whorl, and Composite. Once the difference between these four types has been explained, the most uninformed beginner can distinguish between them.

But in a large collection such as that at Scotland Yard there are thousands of specimens of each type. About sixty per cent of the whole collection are Loops alone. One Loop bears a superficial resemblance to another Loop; they differ only in their details. Yet they have to be classified each in their respective sub-division and that quickly, and without risk of error. How is it done?

Let us take the Loop first, and see how this primary division is sub-divided; what are its essential features, or "fixed points"; and how they are used in the work of classification.

The Outer Terminus. A Loop may be defined by saying that some of the ridges make a backward turn, but without twist. The main stream—it is helpful in this connection to imagine that the lines are those of running water—branches off at one point, and becomes two smaller streams, one of which turns or doubles back and makes a loop.

If you will refer to Fig. 1 this will be made clear.

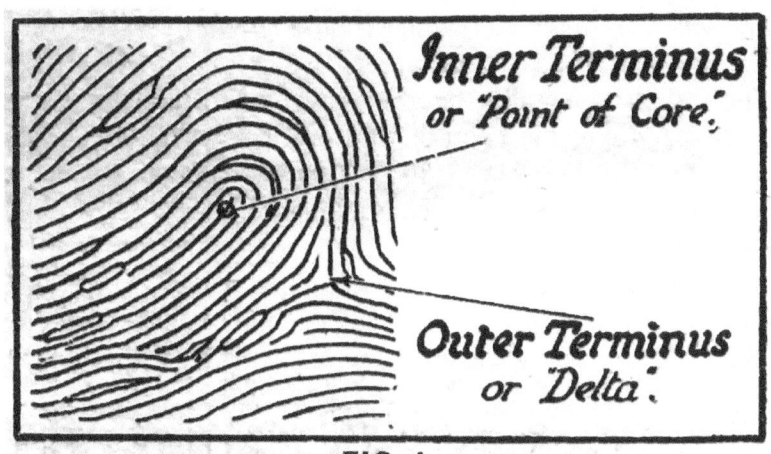

FIG. I.
Showing the " Fixed Points " of the primary " Loop " type.

In a Loop—as in the other primary types—there are present certain fixed points on which classification is based.

These are the Inner Terminus (or Point of Core) and the Outer Terminus (or Delta). These are both shown in Fig. 1.

The Outer Terminus may be formed in two ways. First, by the branching-off of a single ridge, like a letter Y, and second, by the sudden opening out at an angle of two lines that had hitherto run parallel.

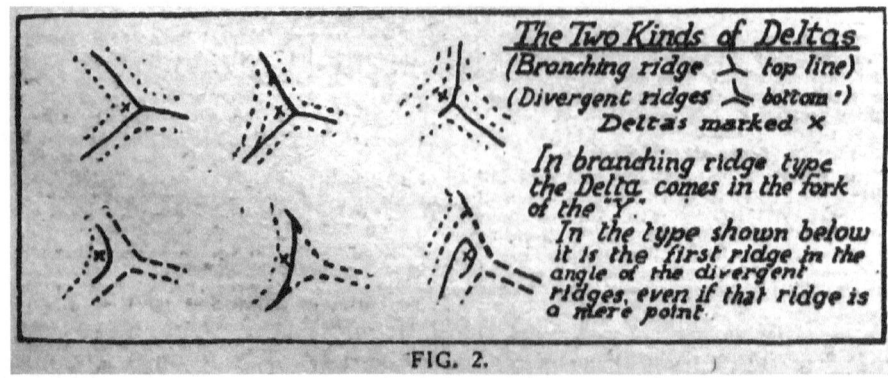

The Two Kinds of Deltas
(*Branching ridge* ⅄ *top line*)
(*Divergent ridges* ⅄ *bottom*.)
Deltas marked ✗

*In branching ridge type
the Delta comes in the fork
of the "Y".
In the type shown below
it is the first ridge in the
angle of the divergent
ridges, even if that ridge is
a mere point.*

FIG. 2.

The diagram (Fig. 2) showing that part of the finger-print containing the Outer Terminus, indicates both methods of forming it. The Outer Terminus in each case is marked X, and the adjacent ridges are dotted.

In the first case the fork of the Y is the Outer Terminus (or Delta). In the second the Outer Terminus is the next ridge in front of the fork, whether this ridge is a mere point, or part of another ridge.

The Inner Terminus.

The other essential "fixed point" is the Inner Terminus, sometimes known as the Point of the Core. This occurs at what might be termed the other extremity of the ridge-stream, and is shown in Figs. 1 and 4, marked by a small circle in each case.

The cores differ in the showing the various types.

In Loops they end in one or more lines (called "rods")—A, B, and C, Fig. 3; or in a line bending back on itself, known as a "staple," presumably from the article of ironmongery which it resembles in shape. (D, Fig. 3.)

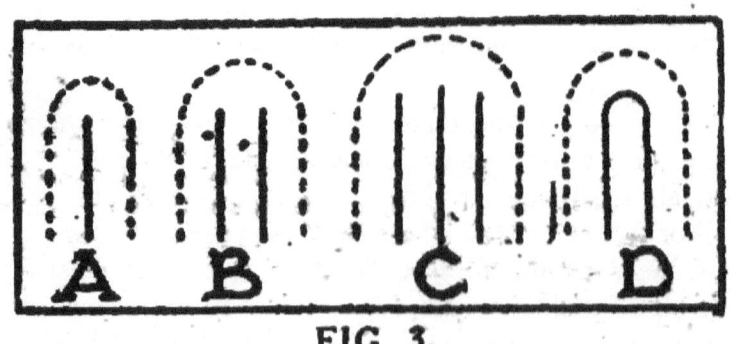

FIG. 3.

In Whorls the core is usually circular or oval in form, and the point of the core in that case is the centre of the inner ring.

Some Whorls, however, tend to be spiral in form, and appear to revolve from a centre. In these instances the points of the core (Inner Termini) are the spots where the spiral begins to revolve. The print on the left-hand side of the heading to this article is a whorl of this type, and the point of the core will be obvious.

This is not particularly relevant just now, as it is with Loops we are concerned at present, so it will be fully dealt with later on.

The Inner Terminus of a Loop is shown in simplified form in Fig. 4. The dotted line in these diagrams represents the first ridge which surrounds the core. The point of the core (Inner Terminus) is determined in this way:

When there is only one rod (A, Fig. 3) the top of this is, of course, the point of the core. When there is any other uneven number—three, for instance, as in the left hand specimen in Fig. 4— the top of the centre one is the point of the core.

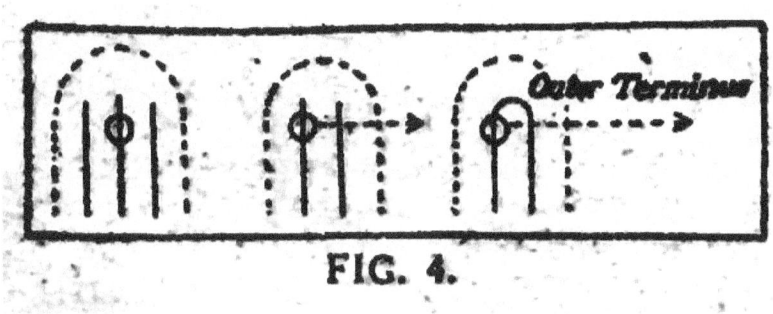

FIG. 4.

When there is an even number—two or more—the two centre ones are considered to be joined by an imaginary line, like a staple. And of these two rods the top of the one farther from the Outer Terminus is the Inner Terminus.

Ridge Counting.

The same rule applies in the case of the staple. In this instance the Inner Terminus is the shoulder of it farthest from the Outer Terminus.

A glance at Fig. 4 will make this plain.

The Inner and Outer Termini are not only outstanding features of a finger-print, but are used as starting places on which to base further classification.

The individual character of any given print is further decided by the methods of counting the ridges between the Delta and the Point of the Core.

A straight line is accurately drawn from one point to the other, and by means of the needle-pointed appliance illustrated in last week's article the ridges are carefully counted.

It should be specially noted, by the way, that neither the Inner nor the Outer minus are to be included in the count, but only the ridges which cut the line between them.

For instance, the simplified diagram in Fig. 1 shows a Loop with a count of eight ridges, excluding the Delta and the Point of the Core. Here, however, about half of the ridges have been omitted for the sake of simplicity; in an actual print the number might be anything from half a dozen to twenty or so.

So much for the "fixed points," the almost invariable essential characteristics and jumping off places in the great majority of prints.

"Ulnar" and "Radial."

Now for another differentiation in the primary class of Loops.

Loops are split up into four divisions according to the downward slope of the ridges.

If you will examine your finger-tips you will most probably find that at least one on each hand is a Loop. This is the commonest of the four primary types, and it is rare to find it altogether absent.

If you will compare the two corresponding fingers side by side— the two forefingers if they happen to be Loops—you will almost certainly find that the general slope of the ridges is in opposite directions. That is, the downward slopes either converge or are in an outward direction. It is very improbable that they will be parallel, that is to say, both flowing either to the right or to the left.

This fact has made it very convenient for the extra-large proportion of finger-prints which come under the heading of Loops to be further broken up.

It would have been easy to have split them into two under the headings of "Left-hand Downward Slope" and "Right-hand Downward Slope." But Sir Edward Henry, when he devised the very ingenious classification system which is now in use in practically every police force in the world, went one better than that, and, at the same time, prevented confusion between pairs of prints liable to be very similar.

He has divided them into four instead of two. They are divided into two classes for each hand, according to whether the ridges tend to the right or the left.

In the case of a print taken from a right-hand digit, those Loops in which ridges slope downward to the left in the print are called Radial Loops. If the ridges slope to the right, the Loop is an Ulnar Loop.

In the left hand this is reversed.

FIG. 3. By way of example: If the print shown in Fig. 1 was from a finger on the right hand, it would be a Radial Loop. If from a left hand digit, it would be Ulnar.

The symbols used at Scotland Yard for these four classes are as follows:

On RIGHT Hand: ULNAR\ RADIAL/

On LEFT Hand: ULNAR/ RADIAL\

At first sight this may appear rather complicated, but it is not so in reality. Once the idea has been grasped it is easy to make the distinction, but to obviate confusion a simple method has been devised to help the memory.

Here again a glance at the accompanying sketch will make the thing clear.

Fig. 5 shows a pair of hands, left and right, palms downward on the table. Above each of them is a pair of Loops, shown in simplified form.

In both hands the Loops whose downward ridges slope TOWARDS the little finger are Ulnar; those whose ridges slope AWAY from the little finger are Radial.

Therefore if a given print is described as either Ulnar or Radial it can be seen at a glance which hand it came from by the direction of the sloping ridges.

It will be seen that this is so because the signs \ and / not only indicate the general direction of the ridges, but are different in meaning for each hand. In a right hand / means Radial, and in a left it means Ulnar.

For the reasons already stated—the prevention of confusion between similar pairs of loops, etc.—it is very necessary to have the distinction between Ulnar and Radial well understood, as in correct classification a lot depends upon it. It has therefore been dwelt on at length.

Although the point at first sight seems somewhat obscure, the diagram should make the two terms quite easy to understand. (Another interesting Finger Print Article next week.)

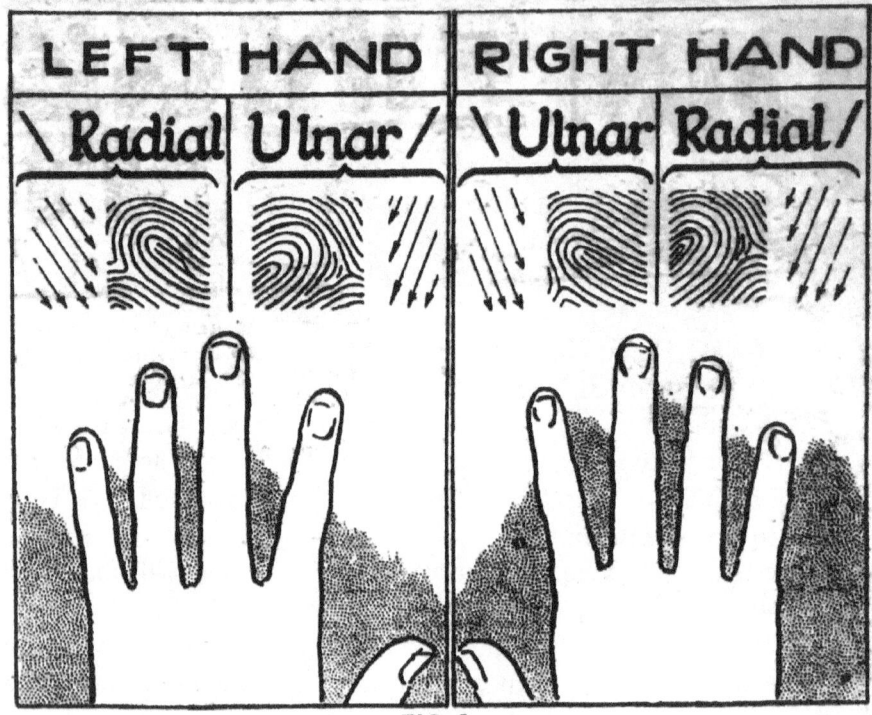

FIG. 5.

This sketch graphically explains the "Ulnar" and "Radial" rule as applied to loops. If a print from a finger or thumb of either hand has the general direction of its ridges TOWARDS the little finger when that hand is placed palm downwards on the table, it is an "Ulnar" loop. If the ridges slope AWAY from it, it is a "Radial."

FIG.. 5

This sketch graphically explains the "Ulnar" and "Radial" as applied to loops. If a print from a finger or thumb of either hand has the general direction of its ridges TOWARDS the little finger when that hand is placed palm downwards on the table, it is an "Unlar" loop. If the ridges slope AWAY from it, it is a "Radial."

ODDS and ENDS

A Bill has just been passed into law by the Belgian Senate which will allow married women holding a doctor's diploma in law to practise as lawyers— but only when their husbands' consent is first obtained.

-

A new form of theft has been discovered by certain Parisian thieves. In several cases the valuable platinum points of lightning conductors on the roofs of buildings have been sawn off and large amounts realised by their sale to crook receivers.

-

Book-borrowers who fail to return the loaned volumes are now liable to imprisonment on conviction in the Russian Bolshevik courts.

-

The taking of drugs has reached such a pitch in Paris lately that a special force of detectives has been created to combat the dope-peddlers' activities.

-

In English law a policeman has the right to search any person whom he arrests on a reasonable suspicion of felony.

-

In thieves' slang the term used to describe the practice of stealing washing hung out to dry is "snowdropping."

-

An imperturbable Chinese laundryman, when dangerously wounded after an attempted hold-up at his laundry, declined to receive treatment at the hospital. He said "Too much washee!" and went back to work.

-

A burglar in Paris, after committing four burglaries on one night, left his pocket-book containing identity papers in the last house visited. One of the papers showed his criminal record, and that he had been previously arrested nine times. This curious oversight led to his prompt arrest for the tenth time.

-

A prisoner in the city gaol, Seattle, Washington, picked up a diamond tie-pin in the room where a police dance had been held. He handed in his find to the prison officials, and as a reward for his honesty the remainder of his sentence was cancelled, and he was allowed to go free.

-

Racially, the Chinese are proved by actuarial experts to be the most honest. Anglo-Saxons come next.

-

In consequence of suspicions directed against a certain American police chief, some U.S. state troopers were disguised as burglars. The police chief was afterwards arrested by the "burglars" and charged with attempting to extort money.

-

Statistics compiled by Scotland Yard show that the sum of £121,185 2s. 4d. was raised by means of 365 street collections for charity during 1921—one for every day in the year. The average cost of collection was about two shillings in the pound. When the police are of opinion that the cost of collection is high, they are empowered to refuse permits for future collections.

-

The police authorities at Rome are considering the use of bombs by the constabulary for dealing with riotous crowds. The bombs —a new invention, explode with a vivid flash, causing temporary blindness.

-

To cope with the dope traffic, New York's police organisation has created a body of detectives known as the Narcotic Squad.

-

For reasons of economy, about twenty-five industrial and reformatory schools in this country are being closed.

-

During the last twelve months no fewer than 170 public executions for high treason have been carried out in the main square of Angora, the capital of the Turkish Nationalists—over two per day.

-

A committee of judges and benchers of the Inns of Court have recently decided that women barristers are to wear wigs, and that their costume when in court shall be modelled on male barristers' as far as is practicable.

The Story of a Magnificent Piece of a Magnificent Detective Work

An enthralling, vividly-written account of the mysterious affair at a Treasury Office in Iowa, U.S.A., involving an actual adventure of Allan Pinkerton, America's real-life Sexton Blake.

The Story of a Magnificent Piece of pure Detective Work.

An enthralling, vividly-written account of the mysterious affair at a Treasury Office in Iowa, U.S.A., involving an actual adventure of ALLAN :: :: PINKERTON, America's real-life Sexton Blake. :: ::

A Baffling Case—The Details of the Crime—The Victim Recovers—Pinkerton's Detective Stroke—The Ruse, and How It Succeeded—The Real Criminal Discovered

IT is safe to say that the following affair is almost incredible.

To narrate the story of Benton Emery and the plundered Treasury safe is to invite disbelief. It is true, nevertheless; it is one of those cases in which truth is indeed stranger than fiction.

Were a writer of detective stories to invent such a plot, his work (if it ever got into print) would be received with grins of incredulity. He would be taxed with having too much invention; or too little of it; or would be thought to be pulling the public's leg,

Allan Pinkerton, the pioneer private inquiry agent who investigated and proved all the facts, himself described it as "one of the strangest incidents in my detective career." Although his career was a long one, and he handled thousands of cases during it, few surely could have been stranger than the Benton Emery affair.

Here are the facts, briefly set forth as Pinkerton himself divulged them.

One day in December, 1870, a man walked into Pinkerton's office and requested an interview. He was the president of one of the national banks of Chicago, and he reported that an official who was stationed in a small village of Iowa had been attacked and nearly killed by robbers, and that a sum approximating £3,200 had been stolen from the safe in the Treasury office. The caller had, he said, been requested to place the affair in the hands of Allan Pinkerton by a correspondent of the bank's in the same county of Iowa as the branch office was situated.

This was the first report of what afterwards developed into one of the most baffling mysteries the detective ever investigated.

Having no further details, all Pinkerton could do then was to despatch one of his most capable and trusted men to the place, with general instructions to keep his eyes open and find out what he could. He himself, as was his habit when the growth of his detective agency brought in more business than he personally could cope with, remained at the central office, in touch with all his men, and ready to bring his better equipped mentality to bear on any problems their reports might contain.

The Discovery.

The subordinate's name was Hanlon, a clever Irish-American who had had experience in such cases before, and had something of specialist's knowledge of them.

The result of his first investigations were telegraphed to his chief within a few days. What he had discovered was this:

On the night of the ninth of December a man named Newcomb had gone to the courthouse for the purpose of purchasing a bond. The courthouse was a sort of rendezvous of the county officials, and the deputy treasurer, Benton Emery, was usually to be found in the treasurer's office during the evenings till about nine o'clock.

As soon as he entered the place the visitor saw it was in darkness. He struck a light and found on the floor the body of a man, covered with blood, and apparently on the point of death. On the floor also was the lamp, smashed, accounted for the room having been in darkness. Also, chairs and other furniture were scattered about, some of it broken. Everything pointed to a severe and prolonged struggle having occurred.

The reason for it was soon explained, for the next thing Newcomb saw was the safe, the door open, and the interior empty of the bonds and money it should have contained. All around it on the floor were scattered papers and parcels, obviously thrown madly aside by the robbers when they reified the safe.

Newcomb turned the dying man over, and saw that it was the deputy treasurer, Benton Emery.

Assistance was procured, and Emery was carefully conveyed to his home. Here he hovered between life and death for three or four days. But he had a story to tell, and with strange persistence he hung on to life, and, despite his terrible wounds, he proved the doctors wrong and lived to tell of what had happened on the fateful evening.

Benton Emery's Story.

Just after dusk, he said, two men had entered his office and asked to be supplied with some Revenue stamps to the value of about £1. A £20 bill was tendered in payment, and Benton Emery took up a magnifying glass to examine it—a necessary course, as there were then many spurious bills in circulation.

It was genuine, however, and he opened the safe for the purpose of getting change.

Directly the door swing open he was seized from behind. One of the men grasped his throat and threatened him with a dagger. The choking fingers prevented him making any sound, but he put up a fight.

He clutched the dagger by the blade, but the man holding it drew it through his hand, so that his thumb was nearly severed at the ball.

The pressure on his windpipe was increased and his struggles became feebler. He felt his strength going, and was compelled to relax his efforts somewhat. About the last thing he knew was that he received several stabs in the side. When next he woke to consciousness it was in bed, and to see the doctors round him.

That was the gist of his story, and everything went to corroborate it. There was a gash on his hand, obviously caused by the dagger being drawn across it; round the heart were four deep wounds, caused apparently by a dagger-like instrument; the throat was also wounded; and there was a terrible gash in the scalp which laid bare the skull beneath.

As regards the safe, it had already been discovered that a large sum of about £3,200 and several packets containing smaller amounts, were missing.

Emery was shown two tough-looking criminals, manacled and strongly guarded.

Emery Helps in the Search.

The officials and Pinkerton's were alike convinced that a daring robbery had been committed, and murder attempted. No other theory could account for the terrible wounds that the deputy-treasurer had received.

That was the state of affairs when Pinkerton—with his subordinate Hanlon on the spot—commenced his investigations. It should be mentioned, by the way, that he was not approached in the matter for some weeks after the robbery, and that when his lieutenant reached the spot Benton Emery had so far recovered from his ordeal as to be on his feet again, and to be taking an active interest in hunting down the criminals.

He was constantly to be seen with Hanlon, Pinkerton's "operative," and aided him with advice that came of wide knowledge of the locality and its people. Benton Emery was a very wealthy man, and it was proved that he had been dabbling in no speculations that might have induced him to stage a robbery so as to obtain money. So he was ruled out of the possible suspects—apart, of course, from being already exonerated on account of having been nearly murdered.

Hanlon, and Pinkerton at headquarters, had a very difficult job to tackle. Every possible clue was investigated—with the same result.

Nor did the famous private detective's great knowledge of the criminals of the day help him. He knew the character of their work, each and every one of them; but on this "job" there was no trade mark of theirs. Besides which, in following up this line of investigation, he proved conclusively that none of the old hands had been anywhere in the vicinity.

The village, too, was so small that the advent of a strange face into it would have been sure to have attracted remark, and had been no strangers near the place for weeks before the robbery.

The Only Slender Clue

The only inference was that the crime must have been the work of somebody in the village itself. Hanlon was told to work on this theory, and he certainly did so.

Everybody was questioned; the history and antecedents of every man and youth in the district was gone into very thoroughly, their financial affairs investigated, and everything relevant—and a lot irrelevant—was brought to light.

The result remained the same—not a clue of any sort discoverable.

But Pinkerton did not know when he was beaten, and told his man to stick to it, which he accordingly did.

He sent his chief report after report of fresh investigations made—all leading nowhere.

Sitting in his office at headquarters, far away from the scene of the crime, these reports were all Allan Pinkerton had to aid him in unravelling the tangle. The fact that the affair was ultimately elucidated by their slender help goes to show the quality of Pinkerton's skill as a real-life detective.

In giving his account of the mystery, he shows how, in going through and through these reports in the faint hope that he might see in them some slight indication of the real solution, he came to this sentence:

"Mr. Emery is ceaseless in his efforts to assist me, but seems to be very much opposed to my going so hard upon the people of the village, as he constantly insists that it was done by professional robbers from a distance."

The detective's mind could not get free from this paragraph. Try as he would his eyes kept going back to it, and his brain insisted on hammering out the question. "Why?"

What Was the Motive?

Why was Emery so considerate about his fellow-townsmen, seeing that every other clue had been worked out without success? Why was he so certain that it had been done by criminals from a distance?

Pinkerton could not help feeling at last that behind all this there was a motive. But what was the motive?

These half-suspicions, he realised, were unjust to the man who had already been nearly murdered as his share of the affair. But they persisted, and Pinkerton decided to at least test them.

He accordingly telegraphed to Hanlon in code to watch every expression and mood of the deputy treasurer, and to report anything he did, whether suspicious or not, without, of course, betraying to the man what he was doing.

Pinkerton had further food for thought when the resulting reports came in. Hanlon stated that Emery seemed to be restless and worried; he was in a listless condition, and any plan proposed for seeking or investigating a fresh clue appeared to make him excited and nervous. Also, he had expressed a desire that the operation should be abandoned.

The inference was obvious, and the question arose: "Whom was he shielding?"

Pinkerton decided to get that question answered, and to this end adopted a ruse. He arranged for an anonymous letter to be sent to Hanlon from a city called Dubuque, some distance from the village.

This letter stated that the writer knew that two suspicious characters could be found in a certain place in Dubuque, and that he had good reason to believe they were the couple concerned in the robbery and attempted murder. Their descriptions exactly tallied with those Benton Emery himself had given of the men.

Pinkerton snatched away the covering from a large wall-mirror.

Hesitations

Emery, together with Pinkerton's man, started out for Dubuque, so as to identify and arrest the criminals.

The victim of the robbery, however, could hardly be induced to start. He made all manner of excuses. He said that he had no faith in anonymous letters, and that the whole thing would be a false alarm.

113

Hanlon, acting on his chief's instructions, said that if the suspicious characters were found, he would certainly arrest them on some trivial charge and take them back with him.

Emery was loud in his protestations against this. He seemed overwhelmed by the complications such an action would result in, and urged the injustice of it.

At last before they had quite reached their destination, he flatly refused to go any further, on the grounds that, even if the real robbers were put in front of him, he would be unable to identify them.

In short, it was plain that Emery knew as well as Hanlon that the men who robbed the Treasury were not in Dubuque. It was equally plain that he knew the real robbers. If so, why was he seeking to hide them?

A report of what had happened confirmed Pinkerton in his first suspicion, and indicated that the deputy-treasurer had guilty knowledge of the crime in some way. It also decided him on his next move.

He would have him come to his office, where he could study him, form judgment on him, and determine whether or not his incredible suspicions were really justified.

What is the Explanation?

In spite of Emery's curious conduct, Pinkerton could not imagine what connection he had with the affair. Possibly he was being blackmailed by the thieves on account of some former indiscretion. Possibly they had "squared" him with a share of the loot—but a share of £3,200 to a wealthy man like Emery would have been no attraction. So far, there was nothing to set off against the mystery but vague suspicion. He determined to apply a second test.

Pinkerton wired to Hanlon to come at once to his office with Mr. Emery.

He stated that the men they had had word of in Dubuque were informed of the move against them, that they had fled to Chicago, and that they had been arrested by Pinkerton's men in that city. They were, the telegram concluded, being detained at Pinkerton's, and the presence of Emery was essential to identify them.

The next morning Hanlon and Benton Emery arrived.

The latter was shown two tough-looking criminals. They were manacled and strongly guarded. Their general appearance certainly accorded with a charge of attempted murder

Pinkerton noticed with keen, if concealed, interest that the victim was looking far more concerned than the captives. His startled looks as he beheld the pair, and his embarrassed and furtive manner suggested that he himself was the would-be murderer, rather than being the man who had been half-murdered.

The detective chief ventured to Emery the belief that they had got the right men at last. Emery replied that he hoped so. And this was all that could be got out of him, except a mumbled statement that he could not swear to their being the right men. He looked thoroughly scared.

They were not the "right men," as it happened, for they were a couple of Pinkerton's own detectives, disguised and instructed in their parts, which they acted with very convincing skill.

But Benton Emery did not know this, and, in the meantime, he had other things on his mind.

He had been invited by Pinkerton into the chief detective's private office, where the trend of the latter's remarks were making him feel distinctly uneasy.

After a little fencing, Pinkerton came out with the abrupt question:

"What would you say, Mr. Emery, if I should tell you that, although you fail to identify the parties outside, I now have the perpetrator of the crime in this office?"

Emery's face became suddenly white.

"Yes," continued Pinkerton, "and what would you say if I were to show you the man in this very room?"

"Where—where?" gasped the visitor, gazing with panicky eyes in every direction.

"There—there! Look at him!"

Pinkerton rose from his chair quickly and uncovered something that stood in one corner. It was a large wall-mirror, and in it was reflected the staring white face of Benton Emery.

He gazed at the glass as if the ghastly presentment of his own terror-stricken face was hypnotising him.

At last he wrenched his eyes away.

"For Heaven's sake, Mr. Pinkerton," he said, "tell me! You don't mean—"

"You know what I mean, Emery!" replied the investigator, "You know it! Now, out with the truth!"

Emery, seeing his secret discovered, came out with it.

His story makes about as strange revelation as has ever been made to a detective, real or fictitious.

Emery, as already stated, was a rich man, and beyond the reach of want for the remainder of his life. To him the money in the safe was a paltry amount.

Yet, for some obscure reason which Psychologists are best fitted to answer, he had himself taken the money, and had buried it under the pavement in front of his office.

To disguise this fact, he had inflicted on himself the terrible dagger wounds from which he had nearly died, first having broken up the office furniture, scattered papers about, and staged all the evidences of a hand-to-hand death struggle.

The reason he suggested for having taken to this apparently insane course of action was that he had been so long in the habit of being shut in the office at nights with substantial sums of money in the safe, that he had been obsessed with the idea of being robbed.

He was constantly revolving this idea in his head, and at length it grew upon him, assuming uncontrollable dimensions. Finally, he decided, for want of a real robber, to rob himself.

How well he did it has been shown. He was not mad—Or, at least, the medical science of those days did not regard him as mad—and he was required to answer for his "crime." Had he lived in these more enlightened times, he would undoubtedly have been the subject of close examination by mental experts, but as it was, he was taken back by Hanlon to the village he had left the day before as a reputable citizen, a disgraced man.

The money was found under the pavement as he had said.

This story, sad as it was, was to have a sadder ending, for two days after his arrival he committed suicide, unable to bear the shame and disgrace.

Thus concluded a really remarkable affair, and one that would for ever have remained a mystery had it not been for the insight of Allan Pinkerton.

Miles from the spot, and with nothing but an assistant's report to guide him, he deduced the complicity of the supposed victim, and by means of a simple trick translated suspicion into certainty, laying bare what would otherwise have never been discovered, and proving the truth of something almost unbelievable.

The criminal's lot daily becomes a harder one! The latest discouragement to lawbreaking is provided by a recent decision on the part of the heads of the Chicago police.

It has been decided to equip every policeman on duty in the city with a portable wireless telephone outfit. On receipt of the news of a crime at headquarters the news will be simultaneously transmitted to every constable, and in a flash the net will be spread far and wide to catch the feet of the escaping criminals.

The telephone receiver will be carried in the policeman's pocket, and the antennæ of the miniature installation will be hidden in the lining of his coat. A buzzer, which forms part of the outfit, will give the alarm in an unmistakable manner.

In addition to this safeguard—which has been adopted mainly to check the activities of the gangs of motor bandits with which American cities are at present infested, a number of speedy light cars, carrying a dozen policemen, have been arranged for. These also carry wireless telephone installations, though of a more powerful type, and which can both send and receive messages.

The latter idea has also been adopted by the Parisian police, who will use their wireless-equipped cars for combating the apache peril, for reporting accidents, for asking headquarters to send reinforcements, etc.

Next Week: "CANADA BILL," the Gipsy Crook.

Its Men and Its Methods.

By George Dilnot

THE WORK OF THE WORLD-FAMED C.I.D.

In last Thursday's DETECTIVE MAGAZINE the well-informed author of this series told of the organisation and work of Scotland Yard's Criminal Investigation Department. He told how, by the use of the latest scientific methods and all the resources of an unrivalled experience, the net is cast far and wide, and how the official detective gets on the trail of his unknown quarry. Here he takes the reader further, and reveals the steps that lead to his ultimate arrest.

ONCE the hounds have glimpsed their quarry it is almost hopeless for him to attempt to escape. His description, his photograph, specimens of his writing, are spread broadcast for the aid of the public in identifying him wherever he may hide. A conspicuous case of this was in the recent Bournemouth murder case, in which facsimiles of the telegrams in the murderer's handwriting were reproduced in almost every newspaper is the country, and in many abroad, so far, unfortunately, without success.

Men watch the big railway stations, outgoing ships are kept under surveillance, for the C.I.D. has two or three staff men resident in many parts. They are also maintained at ports like Boulogne and Calais.

The co-operation of the provincial and foreign police is obtained, and the wide publicity of the newspapers.

The whole-heartedness with which the public throws itself into a hunt of this kind has disadvantages as well as advantages. A score of times a day people will report someone "very like" the wanted man as seen almost simultaneously in a score of different places. All these reports have to be immediately investigated.

And with the search for the culprit the ceaseless search for evidence goes on.

It is no use to catch a murderer if you cannot adduce proof against him. The enthusiasm of the investigators is not called forth by a blood-hunt. It is all a part of the mechanism. The C.I.D. and its members are merely putting through a piece of business quite impersonally.

"A murder has been committed," they say in effect. "We have caught the person we believe responsible, and this is the evidence. It does not matter to us what is happening now. The jury are responsible."

Undramatic

It once fell to the lot of the writer to see an arrest for a murder with which the world rang. The merest novice in stage management could have obtained a better dramatic effect; the arrest of a drunken man by an ordinary constable would have had more thrill.

It was in a street thronged with people passing homewards from the city. A single detective waited on each pavement. Presently one of them lifted his hat, and the other crossed over. They fell into step each side of a very ordinary young man. "Your name is so-and-so," said one. "We are police officers, and we should like an explanation of one or two things. It may be necessary to detain you." A cab stopped, the three got into it, and as it drove away there were not two people among the thousands in the street who knew that anything out of the ordinary had happened.

That is typical of the way arrests for great crimes are effected, if possible. Yet, sometimes circumstances force melodrama on the detectives.

Another arrest which was watched by the writer took place at dead of night in a dirty lodging-house in an East End street. A house-to-house search had been instituted by forty or fifty armed detectives. They expected desperate resistance when they found their quarry, and at last they came upon the man they sought sleeping peacefully on a truckle bed.

A giant detective lifted him bodily. A greatcoat was bundled over his nightshirt, and he was sent off as he was, under escort, into the night.

On the Trail.

Primarily, the great function of the police is to prevent crime; secondly, when it has happened, to bring the offender to justice. How do they work? Not by relying on spasmodic flashes of inspiration, but by hard, painstaking work, and, of course, organisation.

Crime is divided into two classes—the habitual and the casual. Every habitual criminal is known. Numbers vary, but at a rough estimate there are 1,000 habitual criminals in London, of whom 700 or so are thieves and perhaps 160 receivers, the remainder being engaged in other forms of crime.

Now, each of these thieves has a distinctive method. A crime occurs. It is reported to the local police-station, and a detective is sent to the scene. Perhaps he is able to say off-hand: "This job was done by so-and-so."

Then, having fixed his man, he sets to work to accumulate evidence. Scotland Yard is reported to, and thence word is sent to every police-station to keep a look-out for Brown or Jones or Smith—that is, if he has left his usual haunts.

Every detective—strange as it may seem, makes it a point to keep on good terms with thieves. It is his business. Sooner or later the man "wanted" is discovered, unless he is exceptionally astute.

There are, of course, a hundred ways of finding the author of the crime. The good detective chooses the simplest. Subtle analysis is all very well, but it is apt to lead to blind alleys. Imagine a case such as occurs every day:

A burglary has been committed and reported to the police. The first steps are automatic.

The divisional detective-inspector in control of the district sets his staff to work. Men get descriptions of the stolen property, and within an hour the private telegraph and telephone wires have carried them to every police-station in London.

The great printing machine of Scotland Yard reels of "Informations" four times a day, and in the next edition the story of the crime is told, and each of the 650 detectives in London, as well as the 20,000 uniformed police, have it impressed upon their minds.

Swift, unobtrusive little green motor-cars carry "Pawnbrokers' Lists" to every police station to be distributed by hand. The "Police Gazette" goes out twice a week to the whole police forces of the British Empire.

Elimination

Every honest market in which the booty can be disposed of is closed. If the thief has been unwary enough to leave a fingerprint it is photographed, and should he be an old hand the records at Scotland Yard show his identity in less than half an hour.

All this is a matter of routine.

It is still "up to" the detectives to find their man. Should there be nothing tangible to act upon, the detectives—who know intimately the criminals in their district, and many out of it will try a method of elimination. "This," they will say in effect, "is probably the work of one of half a dozen men. Let us see who could have done it, and then we shall have something to go on. A. and B. are in prison; C. we know to be in Newcastle, and D. was at Southampton. Either E. or F. is the man."

The personal factor enters into the work here. A detective is expected to be on friendly terms with professional criminals, although he must not be too friendly. The principle can be illustrated by an anecdote of Mr. Froest, the famous detective.

Knowing His Man

Once or twice he had arrested a notorious American crook who was carrying on operations in this country, and whom I will call Smith. In one of his occasional spells of liberty, Smith, who was a reputed murderer in his own country, met Froest. "Say, chief," he drawled, after a little conversation. "I'd just hate to hurt a man like you. I always carry a gun, and there are times when I'm a bit too handy with it. If ever you've got to take me, never do it after six in the evening. I'm a bit lively then."

It is the business of a detective to know thieves. Without an acquaintance with their habits of thought and their social customs he may be lost. The "informant" plays a great part in practical detective work, and the informant, it follows, is often a thief himself. Of the manner in which he is used I shall have more to say later.

So it is among the friends (and enemies) of E. and F. that the detectives set to work. It is a task that calls for tact. E. we will suppose, is at home, and all his movements about the time of the crime are checked and counter-checked. F. has vanished from his usual haunts. This is a circumstance suspicious in itself, but rendered more so by the fact that his wife is uncommonly flush of money.

Often it is harder to connect together legal evidence of guilt than to catch a criminal. The most positive moral certainty is not sufficient to convict a man, and English detectives may not avail themselves of methods in use abroad to bring home a crime to the right person.

Perhaps a detective pays a visit to F.'s wife. With the remembrance of many kindly acts performed by the police during her husband's involuntary absences, she is torn between a stubborn loyalty to him and her wish to be civil to her visitor.

He is sympathetic—cynics may not believe that the sympathy is often genuine—but he has his duty to do. He does not expect her consciously to betray her husband, but his eyes are busy while he puts artless questions. An incautious word, the evasion of a question, may give him the hint he seeks, or, on the other hand, she may be too alert, and his mission may be fruitless.

Meanwhile, a description and photograph of F. have been circulated by what may be called the publicity department of Scotland Yard. It may be even given to the newspapers, for your modern detective realises the advantage of deft use of the Press.

Always Found at Last.

Remember, F. is a known criminal, and even in so vast a place as London no man who is known can hide himself indefinitely. A striking personal instance may be cited.

The writer, in the course of an aimless walk through obscure streets, accompanied by a well-known detective, was greeted by no fewer than eight officers. I believe there is no instance on record of a definite person being "wanted" where the police have failed to find him. He may have escaped arrest for lack of evidence, but he has been found.

The wide-flung net will sooner or later, enmesh F. He may be seen and recognised, or, what is more likely, he will be betrayed by one of his associates.

It does not follow that he will at once be arrested and charged. He may be merely "detained," which means that the police have him in custody for not more than twenty-four hours, at the end of which time he must either be brought before a magistrate or set at liberty. He must not be questioned, but he is given to understand why he is held, and may, if he likes, volunteer a statement.

If any of the stolen property is found on him the matter at once becomes straight forward, and if he is believed to have hidden or disposed of it to any particular person search warrants are procured to bring it to light.

To be continued in next Thursday's Supplement

www.ingramcontent.com/pod-product-compliance
Lightning Source LLC
Chambersburg PA
CBHW031833170626
46807CB00004B/1447